F Vásquez
Vásquez, Juan Gabriel, 1973-
Lovers on All Saints' Day

Lovers on
All Saints'
Day

Lovers on All Saints' Day

STORIES

JUAN GABRIEL VÁSQUEZ

TRANSLATED FROM THE SPANISH

BY ANNE MCLEAN

RIVERHEAD BOOKS

New York

RIVERHEAD BOOKS
An imprint of Penguin Random House LLC
375 Hudson Street
New York, New York 10014

First published in Great Britain in 2015
as *The All Saints' Day Lovers* by Bloomsbury Publishing
Originally published in Spain in 2008
as *Los amantes de Todos los Santos* by Alfaguara
Copyright © 2005, 2008 by Juan Gabriel Vásquez
English translation copyright © 2015 by Anne McLean

Library of Congress Cataloging-in-Publication Data

Vásquez, Juan Gabriel, date.
[Short stories. Selections. English]
Lovers on All Saints' Day : stories / Juan Gabriel Vásquez ;
translated from the Spanish by Anne McLean.
p.   cm.
ISBN 978-1-59463-426-0
I. Vásquez, Juan Gabriel, *Los amantes de Todos los Santos*. English.   II. Title.
PQ8180.32.A797A2   2015   2015004286
863'.64—dc23

Printed in the United States of America
1   3   5   7   9   10   8   6   4   2

Book design by Gretchen Achilles

FOR MARIANA

Contents

Lovers on All Saints' Day

Hiding Places

I DIDN'T LEAVE BELGIUM much during that season. I spent the time observing the people of the Ardennes and participating in their activities, and then learning to write what I'd seen in such a way that as little of it as possible would be squandered. In February, a Colombian magazine commissioned me to write an article about a certain Parisian bookshop. French trains went directly to Paris from Liège, but they'd gone on strike two weeks earlier and there was no resolution in sight. So I had to take an old orange train from Aywaille station—a switch in every second car allowed passengers to control the heating—a green one from Liège, and spend the night in the house of a couple of friends in Brussels, in order to catch the first direct train to Paris the next morning. I arrived at the bookshop, stayed there for several days lending a hand as an occasional assistant, and wrote my article. But what happened during the night I spent in Brussels will haunt me forever.

Philippe came to pick me up at the main station, the most inhospitable of the three possible terminals for Liège trains.

He was wearing a plaid beret and thick-framed glasses, which he took off to hug me, and on both sides of his nose were red marks from the weight of them. Philippe and Claire had been married the summer before; he was then (at the time of my ill-timed visit) an out-of-work actor. According to what Claire had told me over the phone, he was going through a rough patch: a good contract for a French film had just been canceled due to lack of funding; his first wife was threatening to sue if he didn't hand over half the value of the house in Zaventem, where they'd lived before separating. I didn't talk to him about any of this, because we didn't have that kind of rapport, but in his face—on certain occasions when I asked a polite question, in the grimace with which he waited for a light to change—I could read his preoccupation. We parked right in front of 287 Rue du Noyer; we smelled freshly baked bread as we got out of the car, and this odd fact (it was four in the afternoon) gave us something to talk about during the following uncomfortable minutes. They were uncomfortable because Claire wasn't there: she spent the afternoons in her studio and she had asked me to meet her after seven, to see her latest works and have dinner with her and the people with whom she shared the workshop. They were uncomfortable also because of the incident with the flowers, which in another place, in other circumstances or backed by a different past, might have struck me as slightly odd or banal. On the rough wooden table that served as both dining table and ironing board there was an arrangement of Spanish azaleas with a single sunflower. There was also a typed card: it was the color of raw meat, and around the border were blue watercolor marks. BEST WISHES, it said on the embossed cardboard.

"My father-in-law," said Philippe.

He said *beau-père*, pronouncing the consonants loudly, and smiled with the kind of sarcasm I hadn't thought him capable of. Then he didn't say anything else. The house was tall and narrow (four stories, but each floor was barely four meters wide); Philippe excused himself and began to climb the creaking stairs, one after the other, as if he needed all his patience to get up to the master bedroom on the third floor, above the study where the only phone in the house was, beneath the guest room where I would be spending the night.

THE PREVIOUS AFTERNOON, Philippe's father-in-law, Claire's father, the owner of the house in the Ardennes where I was living temporarily, had come looking for me to take advantage of an unusual circumstance: a late-winter day when the sun was shining.

"The lake is waiting for us," he said. "Hurry, there's not much light left."

Monsieur Gibert did not wait for my answer. He turned

around and the sleeve of his jacket snagged on the angular doorknob. A couple of minutes later, I heard the engine of his four-by-four start up.

The lake was an artificial pond that Monsieur Gibert had built to irrigate a cabbage crop, but the crop failed before it got started, and now the only purpose the lake served was for the occasional distraction of a stubborn retired farmer who stocked it with his own trout, which he later fished. Monsieur Gibert carried a Sander rod in his gloved hand and I followed him, eyes fixed on the green water, on the marshy shore, on the heads of the frogs that shone like floating coins and escaped with small commotions when they saw us coming. I sat down on a beech log. Monsieur Gibert put on his bifocals and moved his skilled fingers over the end of the line and over the three sharp hooks of the lure, silver-plated and hard and shiny in the long rays of the afternoon sun. His left hand closed around the cork handle and his index finger held the line against the rod. He drew his arms to one side, and the momentum of the rod cut through the air and the reel sounded like a child sighing as it spun, and ten meters from the shore the lure broke the surface, with delicacy, as if worried about waking a sleeping frog.

"I want you to keep your eyes open," he said.

"They're open, monsieur."

"At their house," he said. "I want you to notice everything, and then tell me. How they live. If she's all right, if he treats her as she deserves to be treated."

All this he said to me as his right hand turned the handle, reeling the line back in. We weren't looking at each other: we both had our eyes fixed on the sinker and lure sailing toward us like a bullet in slow motion, causing a fragile wake on the surface and emerging upon arrival at the shore. Monsieur Gibert had never been to his daughter's house. They'd invited him once, and he'd come up with some unimaginative and rather banal excuse. I knew this because Claire told me, imitating her father's nasal voice, his falsely solemn gestures. Gibert had never made this impression on me; Claire's complaints made me feel uncomfortable, because I feared her resentments might be contagious. For Claire, everything that happened in her life was the result of what her father had ruined, wasted, or frittered away (emotions, not money).

Gibert stripped tangled plants off the lure. The weeds stuck to the hairs on the back of his hand. He cast again.

"I'm going to tell you something sad," he said. "Philippe's not good for my daughter. I mean, he's a good man, but he has problems."

"But they're not definitive, monsieur. He'll find work."

"Work?"

"He's got a job offer in Montpellier," I lied. "For the summer. They'll pay well, it's street theater."

"His father's a drunk," he said. "His sister's husband beats her up all the time."

He reeled in his lure. He took off two or three little green branches, which looked like asparagus. He cast again.

"His sister, I mean, not Claire. His sister's husband beats his wife."

"Yes, monsieur. I knew what you meant."

"And him, with his first wife, all that . . . Anyway, it's all a big mess. That's what I mean. A chaotic mess."

Then, as he reeled in the lure, the line hardened like a glass tube. "Ah," said Gibert. His hand wound the reel, and two steps away from us a brownish-gray trout appeared, thrashing in the water. Gibert lifted the line, the trout changed color in midair and fell onto the grass on the shore, and the pink flecks on its side looked brighter.

"Here, hold this." Gibert passed me the rod without taking his eyes off the fish. "We'll throw this one back, it's just little."

He began to try to free it from the lure, but the hooks had pierced its cheek and impaled its brown tongue. The blood spread over the silver-plated lure and Gibert's pale fingers. The trout shook, fell to the ground, Gibert squeezed it in his hands again to try to free it, and said keep still, *connasse*, I'm trying to help you. The tongue was bleeding, the lure was stuck in it like an anchor, and I was imagining the intensity of the pain and the miracle of features—eyes, a mouth—in which pain is invisible. I don't usually fish, and maybe that's why I found myself imagining that a knife was going through my tongue, and I would have sworn I felt a surge of pain in my jaw. Little idiot, said Gibert. His thumbnail turned a watery red.

"*Trop tard*," said Gibert. "Too late, filthy creature."

He walked over to the beech logs with the fish still bending in his closed fist, gasping laboriously like an asthmatic. Then Gibert raised his arm and banged down hard against the edge of a stump, and the trout's skull made a flat sound as it hit the bark. Gibert hit it three times, very quickly, and the unechoed crunch of broken bones was clear in the air. The bark of the stump was smeared with scales and blood. The trout, one eye burst and covered in splinters, stopped thrashing.

I SPENT THE AFTERNOON in the Waterstones bookshop near the Bourse, across the street from a peep show. I found a couple of books about the Paris bookshop I was going to visit. They mentioned George Whitman, the owner, and one of them mistakenly said this was the bookshop that had published *Ulysses* in 1922. The other, more useful, said that Whitman (who was not related to the poet, it emphasized) had arrived from California and founded three bookshops before the one that I would visit. It was a small book, almost a pamphlet; I thought I'd read it in the hour and a quarter the train journey from Brussels to Paris took. Then I looked at my watch, left in a hurry, and walked as quickly as the cold, biting February air would let me.

Claire's studio was on Rue Braemt, a street of immigrants in which every second or third building had a Turkish restaurant or a secondhand clothing shop on the ground floor. It was already dark, and only the polished gleam of the neon lights from the shops lit up the quiet street. As I turned the corner, I saw a silhouette in front of the workshop. I had to get very close, almost right in front of her, before recognizing an impatient Claire, who was waiting for me. Or maybe, I thought, it wasn't me she was waiting for.

Her hair was stuck to her temples, as if she'd been sweating. She told me she'd just had a call from Philippe, and after hanging up the phone, she'd cupped her hands under the tap at the workshop sink and splashed her face, as if trying to wake up.

"It's his nephew," she said. "He's been in an accident."

Philippe had only one nephew: his sister's son was an eight-year-old with green eyes who looked nothing like her, but a lot like his father. The only time I met him he confessed that he hated the Flemish language and was never going to learn it.

"What happened?" I asked. "Is it serious?"

"We don't know anything. Go on up, wait for me upstairs. He's on his way here, and I don't think he'd like you to see him right now."

A little kid in baggy trousers went past on a skateboard. Claire didn't even notice him.

"This can't be happening to him," she said. "Not him, not now."

"But Philippe's coming here?"

"Yeah. He won't want you to see him in such a state. Go on up, go, I'll be there in a bit. Poor thing, he's a rotten mess."

The door to her studio was ajar, as she'd obviously rushed out. I thought I caught a whiff of bad eggs, but it might also have been an oil fixative I wasn't familiar with. I thought about the smell and about the word Claire had used, *rotten*, a word barely applicable to a living man. Four neon tubes hung from the high ceiling. On top of a little electric stove, the food Claire was preparing still steamed: stuffed peppers. I took off the lid and the fragrance of the spices mingled with the chemical smell of the fixative and paints. While I waited for Claire, I thought, I could have a look at her canvases. Then I thought she would like to guide me through the paintings when I saw them for the first time, and looking at them without her would be a minor betrayal; so I stretched out on a camp bed covered in wool blankets and picked up a Giacometti book. I couldn't concentrate (part of my attention was trying to hear any sound coming from the street or the ground floor, a crying man, a consoling woman), but I found an old catalog between the pages: in it, Giacometti was asked why the feet of his figures were so big, and he said: *I've always had the impression or sense of the fragility of living beings, as if each moment required an arduous energy to remain upright.* The words struck me as opportunistic and emphatic, an artist's pose. I was involved in these ridiculous imaginings when Claire arrived.

"They don't know anything. And he's very confused. The boy was out for a drive with a couple of friends and the father of one of them. Nothing happened to any of them. Just him."

"But what happened?" I asked.

"They were on the highway. Or not, maybe that's what Philippe thinks. But maybe they were on a mountain road. Why him?"

"Who?"

She looked up and the neon was like powder on her nose. "What do you mean, who?" she whispered, and I realized we were on the brink of a serious misunderstanding. I wanted to say there was an injured child and saying *Why him?* could refer to Philippe but also to the boy. Then I understood I could not speak those words.

"Nothing," I said. "Never mind."

"Poor Philippe, his poor family. I swear, they have such bad luck, it's as if they're cursed."

The intercom buzzed just then. Claire lifted the receiver, said hello to someone with sudden politeness. "Come on up," she said, and pressed a button with an image of a key on it.

"They're here. Shit, now I don't know if I want to see them."

"Tell them what happened."

"It's too late. They've come all this way. They live really far away, I asked them to come and they came. . . ."

"Whatever you say. Can I ask you something?"

Claire opened the door. From downstairs came the voices of her friends who were on their way up.

"Why didn't you go with him?"

"Because he didn't want me to go with him. Because he's always wanted to protect me."

And then she added: "At least, that's what he tells me." The voices on the stairs kept approaching. I asked her what she meant by that, if she didn't believe Philippe's reasons. It was as if she were choking on a marble.

"It's possible he doesn't do it to protect me," she said. "In his family terrible things have happened, if only you knew, it's as if nothing comes out right for them. But maybe, just maybe, he does it to look out for himself. To get home at night, having seen his sister or his father or whoever, and feel that he's entered another world, that he's safe. I don't know, 'cursed' is a strong word, I feel horrible saying it. But there is something he'd like to hide from. If he takes me to these things, if he lets me go with him and I get soaked in that pain, what hiding place remains for him?"

———

AT ABOUT TEN we walked back to Claire's house. The wind had dropped and the streetlights cast shadows of bare branches. We skirted a park and a basketball court. I noticed that the hoops didn't have nets and then I saw the nets piled up on the concrete bleachers. Claire was carrying her phone in her hand, not in a pocket or in her bag, but prepared for it to ring as if urgently answering Philippe's call would alleviate the gravity of events or prevent their consequences. The women she shared her studio with hadn't picked up on anything; we'd discussed Claire's paintings, those pregnant wombs and cartilages and lungs that she was able to bring to life on the canvas. We ate stuffed peppers, and one of her friends (maybe Vera, the one with short hair and a bullfighter's pigtail) pointed out that they resembled the saffron-colored lungs of the paintings. Claire said yes, maybe, that one never knows where shapes and colors come from. But her head was elsewhere, and I was starting to understand that much more than a child's life was at stake: for Claire, something immense and something of her own was at risk that night, as if she'd placed a bet, as if her happiness or ruin depended on a call about another person's fate.

Claire turned on the living room light just long enough to get to the kitchen, and the kitchen light just long enough to fill a plastic IKEA glass with water. She was turning off light switches as she walked through her house as if she were alone there. But the porch light stayed on, waiting for Philippe. We went upstairs without speaking, and on the second floor, Claire took a telephone with a long cord out of the study and left it on the stairs, against the banisters.

"If you come downstairs, be careful not to trip."

"You should put a phone in your bedroom," I said. "Like we do back home."

"Yes, I know. You've told me that before."

I went up to the guest room, on the fourth floor, and found that I could move around without turning on the light, because there was a skylight in the ceiling and the brightness of the street illuminated the outlines of things: the tall headboard of the wooden bed, the wardrobe filled with clean towels. The noise of a nearby party could be felt through the walls, an electronic beat of intense bass notes that echoed in my stomach. I closed my eyes, tried not to listen. The house was dark, but not asleep: it was impossible to forget my wide-awake hostess waiting in that very particular way waiting for a telephone call becomes, such a modern kind of waiting, undoubtedly more anguished than the old waits in romantic novels, because there's nothing more sudden than a phone ringing and there are no other situations where you can go, in less than a second, from well-being to loss. Waiting for someone implies their footsteps before they arrive at the door and waiting for a letter implies the time the envelope spends in our hands before being opened, but a phone call changes the world in an instant: it's not there, and then it is. That's how fast things happen.

I woke up when the phone rang. Somehow I'd fallen asleep, unaware.

I tried to hear, unsuccessfully. The creaky wooden floors prevented me from going down the stairs and listening to the conversation without being discovered. But the silence was not total: Claire's murmuring, thin and soft as tends to happen when we speak to someone who loves us, reached me from afar, through the rude rhythms of the neighbors' music. Claire spoke for three, maybe four minutes. I heard her hang up; I didn't hear her close her bedroom door. I decided to go down: the bathroom, after all, was downstairs. I would have that pretext if I needed one.

I found her sitting on the third step, in front of the open door to her room, with the yellow light from the street barely illuminating the space her compressed body took up on the stairs. She was hugging her knees tight to her chest with her head between her arms, like a beggar in the subway. I put a hand on her shoulder: it was one of the first times I'd touched her (she was or is Belgian, and in spite of our friendship, physical contact was or is unusual and restrained), and Claire raised her head and I saw that she was crying softly, silently.

"The boy died," she said. "Philippe isn't coming home tonight, he's staying with his sister."

I thought of his sister's husband, the man who, according to Monsieur Gibert, mistreated her.

"And her husband . . ."

"Of course, him too. Imagine that guy's rage when he finds out his son is dead."

"They don't live together?"

"It'll be her fault, of course, she sent the child off on the excursion. And the guy's rage. Shit, I'd be scared to death, wouldn't you? Of course, they're all expecting Philippe to be there to protect them. And who's going to protect him? Who's going to comfort him?"

She picked up the receiver and dialed a long number.

"Good evening. I'd like a taxi, please."

THE DRIVER, a Flemish man whose mustache completely covered his mouth, took us to our destination in twenty minutes. Schaerbeek was a neighborhood or suburb I'd been through on the train once or twice, on my way to the airport. Claire had never been to the house we were looking for, but she had an address taken from the invitation list for their wedding. The place just seemed dead: the sidewalks were dull cobblestones, and cars slept on both sides of the road. They were not the latest models: there were Fiats and Renaults from the early eighties, and they all had stickers on the bodywork or the

bumpers, glow-in-the-dark cartoons making love in every possible position, or Flemish phrases—signs of admiration, underlined words—which I didn't understand and had no interest
in deciphering. The taxi pulled over and slowed to a walking
pace. On the dark brick or gray stone walls, beside windows
adorned with lace curtains, the house numbers came into view
and disappeared again. When Claire found the one we were
looking for, she said:

"It's here. Stop, please."

But we didn't get out immediately.

"Are you sure?" I said.

"Of course not. If I were sure, everything would be easier."

"Seven hundred and ninety," said the taxi driver.

"Keep the change," said Claire.

And there we were, the only two people on the empty
street, the collars of our coats turned up (Claire was better protected with her black shawl), frowning at the cold. We looked
up toward the second floor of the house, where the windows
were boxes of silent light.

"It must be there. Philippe has told me about this, the
house is divided into apartments. They don't get along with
the neighbors and the common areas are filthy with grime
because nobody wants to clean them."

It was number 8 Rue Goossens. The eight was wrought
iron, sticking out from the concrete wall. Claire approached
the list of doorbells, her index finger running down the four

names. "Ah," she said, and pressed a button. From the street we could hear an intercom buzzing. Someone I didn't recognize looked out the window; presumably it was the same person whose voice came through the intercom.

"Who is it?"

"Claire Gibert. Claire Vial. Philippe's wife. Good evening, madame."

I'd never heard her introduce herself with her married name. The intercom went silent again and then a new buzz sounded, this time the door. I opened it and we stepped into the dark hallway. The stairs were on the right, and Claire walked toward them as if she knew the way, suddenly in a hurry. I followed her, but I didn't take my hand off the rough handrail for a second.

Philippe was waiting for us in front of the half-closed door to the apartment. He looked at me and it was as if he were blaming me for something. He was wearing a black, unironed shirt, half untucked like an untidy schoolboy. Behind him there was nothing but silence. I had expected murmurs, accusations, disapproval, gossip.

"What are you doing?" he said to Claire.

"I couldn't not be with you," she said. "I love you and I wanted to be with you."

"This isn't . . . she'd rather be alone right now, you know. She'd rather that we—"

Then two doors opened: the neighbors' and the one

Philippe was guarding like a soldier in some fairy tale. The neighbor had a patch over his left eye and was wearing a red dressing gown. The woman who came out behind Philippe had too steady a face to be his sister.

"*Mais, qu'est-ce que vous faites?*" said the neighbor. "Could you not carry on your little chat inside your house?"

"We are inside our house," said Philippe.

"We're in our house," said the neighbor.

"And watch your manners, if you don't want a punch in the face."

"Let's go in," said the woman. "Philippe, it's not worth it."

"*Salauds,*" said the neighbor.

"*Vieux con,*" said Philippe.

"In," said the woman.

She closed the door and some bells jingled (they were copper, tied with red and green thread). Philippe took them down off the door hook.

"That noise gets on my nerves. I don't know how you can stand it."

"Good evening," said Claire.

"Every time it opens, every time you close it."

"Good evening," said the woman. "I'm a friend of the family. Anne. A friend."

We said hello, and I noticed that Claire didn't know quite how to introduce me. This was not the moment to go into details about nationality and profession; I was not going to be of any use to her this time, to break the ice in gatherings of strangers. In the living room, two armchairs and a small sofa were covered with white sheets, and both windows had lace curtains. The woman sitting on top of the sheet, at one end of the sofa, seemed like she hadn't moved in a long time. It was Philippe's sister, the woman whose son had died. Her eyelids were swollen and she had a red mark on her neck. Her head was hanging slightly to one side, her gaze fixed on some point in the sisal rug. Philippe sat down next to her, and Anne, the friend, sat in the other chair. But it was as if Claire and I weren't there, as if we hadn't arrived yet. Claire went over to Philippe; he didn't look at her. He'd put a hand on his sister's knee like someone setting down a cup of coffee. And he did not look at Claire. Not once did he look at her.

No one spoke, the bodies barely moved, and the sound of clothes brushing against the sheets, when that happened, was as clear as a violin in the still air of the room. The only thing I wanted to know was where the dead boy was and if there was anything we could do to help: take care of some of the procedural paperwork, recover the car from the accident site, any of those routine tasks that are terrible because they take us away or distract us from the pain. I said:

"I'm sorry, madame."

Nothing happened. No one looked at me. Philippe's sister did not move her head. And that was when Claire, perhaps tired of standing like a statue at Philippe's side, approached his sister, knelt down at the foot of the sofa, and embraced her. It was a simple gesture, and didn't seem to have any consequences until Claire tried to go back to her place, and the woman's arms surrounded her and kept her there and her voice released a wail, he's dead, Claire, my baby's dead, and I saw the clenched, pale fists against Claire's black shawl. They were heavy hands and they pressed Claire's back and clothes, and the fingers wore no rings and her skin was so fair that blue veins were visible in the faint light. Philippe, sitting beside the two embracing women, looked at the bells he'd put on the coffee table. He picked them up, hung them from one finger, and shook them so it sounded like someone had just come in.

LESS THAN A WEEK LATER, I had to pass through Brussels again, on my way back from Paris, but I was able to change trains at Midi station and continue my trip to the Ardennes without seeing Claire and Philippe. In the house in Aywaille, as soon as I arrived, I began to organize my notes and write the article. About the bookshop's bedroom, I wrote: "It's a child's room, a child who has not visited in a long time. The doors of a wardrobe have been removed in order to fit a little bed inside it, but there are still checked blazers and winter jackets hanging from the rail. There's nothing as lonely as the spectacle of abandoned clothing. It smells of mothballs and ammonia, because the bathroom is right next door. From the portraits, which absorb my attention, I discover that this room belonged, some time ago, to Sylvia Beach Whitman, George's daughter. In the photographs, the little girl plays wearing nothing but a necklace made of flowers or she appears with Baskerville, her German shepherd. It is in fact an altar arranged by George for the adoration of his daughter. There is one thing lonelier than abandoned clothing, and it's a child's room abandoned by the child." As I was writing, I was thinking of Philippe's sister's dead son.

One spring Sunday, three or four weeks after that night, Claire came to Aywaille to talk to Monsieur Gibert. I was pleased to see her, and to see her lightness as she stepped out of the car and the casual air with which we all chatted, standing in the narrow kitchen, warmed by the steam pouring out of the pans and hitting the tiles.

After lunch, Claire and I stayed downstairs. When quite a long time had passed in silence, Claire said:

"Let's go outside. It's hot in here, the windows are all steamed up. Let's go for a little walk."

It was cloudy and the sky looked like rain. We took the path toward the woods, walking on tiptoes between the puddles and fresh mud.

"What a change," said Claire. "I'd never live here, but it's really good to come out here once in a while."

"Nice to breathe fresh air."

"It's so quiet," said Claire. "No parties next door."

"There aren't any people, just animals."

"Philippe's seeing someone," said Claire. "I don't know if my father's told you."

He hadn't told me. But in some obscure way, I'd deduced it after a series of random comments, and had rejected the idea, and soon the idea had come back to worry me. The strange thing was how Claire told me, as if she were talking not about a potential marital disaster but of help found, as if Philippe, rather than going out with another woman—her name was Natasha, she was English and worked for the European Economic Community—were seeing a psychologist.

"She called the house the other day," said Claire. "She didn't even know Philippe was married."

At a fork in the path, where you have to decide whether to go up the hill until you can see Hamoir in the distance or turn right toward the road to Ferrières, we stopped. Claire had gotten distracted as she walked and her tights were soaked and dirty.

"What are you going to do?" I asked.

"Well, I'm going to wait. This is a phase, you know."

And then, as if resuming a conversation we'd interrupted earlier, as if the change of topic wasn't sudden or abrupt:

"When she embraced me, I didn't think about her. I didn't think that hugging me might make her feel better. I thought this embrace was happening to Philippe and me, and we would be the beneficiaries."

She rubbed her hand across her face, looked at it as if her features had become entangled in her palm.

"Maybe all this is a punishment, no? Someone's punishing me for being so egotistical."

We got to the little stone church, a construction the size of a doll's house, where Claire, as a child, used to come and play. It had a rusted iron gate that would no longer budge. It had no Christ, no cross or altar. The interior was nothing but a damp rectangle, the walls devoured by lichen, the concrete floor covered in pine needles. "And what if we prayed?" said Claire; but before I had time to be surprised (Claire was an atheist, as were her parents), she burst out with a short dry laugh. She didn't say anything more until we reached the place where smoke from the chimneys of Hamoir began to come into view. The grass beside the path was too wet for us to sit down, so we stood there, looking at the green carpet that rolled down toward the first buildings. I put my arm around Claire and said:

"When you want to come back, let me know."

"Come back, ah," she sighed. "If it were up to me, I'd stay right here till Judgment Day."

CLAIRE DECIDED NOT TO STAY for dinner: at five in the afternoon the sky was already black, and the prospect of driving to Brussels on her own on the dark, slippery highway seemed exhausting. I walked her to the car and asked her to call us when she got home; I noticed something resembling gratitude in her voice; it was as if she wanted to tousle my hair, as one might do to a brother, but she didn't. I watched her drive away until the red taillights had disappeared. In the living room, Monsieur Gibert had lit a fire; I sat in the upholstered armchair, beside the box of newspaper, and after a while Gibert appeared with an aperitif in hand. I remember that conversation very well, lasting as it did for the entire meal and full of old wartime anecdotes, in particular about the day Gibert rode his bicycle down to Spa and ran into a German soldier younger than he was, just a boy, maybe seventeen years old, and there was in that instant a tremendous understanding in which Gibert wouldn't take his hands off the handlebars to grab his rifle if the soldier didn't reach for his cartridge belt. "Who knows if I'd be alive right now," Gibert said to me, "if one of the two of us hadn't been afraid."

The phone rang then and startled us: it was Claire, probably, Claire who was just getting home and maybe found Philippe not there, or found a note from Philippe lying about his whereabouts or whom he was with. I hoped it wouldn't be, I caught myself hoping with all my might that Philippe was waiting for her when she got home. I stood up to answer when it became obvious that Gibert had no intention of speaking with anyone, not with his daughter, nor with his daughter's husband, who now had a lover; but I must have taken too long, because when I picked up the receiver I didn't hear any voice

but just an even dial tone. And then I stood there, in front of
the telephone, waiting for Claire to phone back, searching
without success for something to say, a phrase that might serve
as an umbrella or a hiding place for her after driving all the
way back to Brussels alone. But when the phone rang—I don't
quite know how to say this—my hands didn't move. I heard it,
I heard the electronic bell and its echo from the house's other
phone, on the second floor, and the cord was brushing against
the sleeves of my shirt; I even played with it, untangling it
carefully, pushing it with my finger so it swayed like a pendulum. But I didn't answer. I imagined it was a friend of the
family calling; they wouldn't be surprised that everyone in
the house was asleep. I imagined someone dialing, getting the
number wrong, from a pay phone, perhaps from a gas station.
It might be a young man, well bundled up, just getting off
work and phoning his girlfriend to ask her to come and meet
him for a drink. I thought about this man; I invented a good
life for him. And after a few seconds the phone stopped ringing, more or less the way a trout stops gasping on the shore.

The All Saints' Day
Lovers

THAT AFTERNOON Michelle came hunting with me. Pierre, the tracker, arrived after lunch. He was wearing his old hat with the feather and a green jacket. His left hand held an invisible rifle. He was impatient, and the yellow laces swung on both sides of his waterproof boots. In the dining room, Michelle swept up the bread crumbs with a plastic-bristled brush, and her blouse slipped off one shoulder, revealing her bra strap.

"Michelle's coming with us," I told Pierre.

"But she's never liked it."

"Exactly," she said. "I'm not going anywhere."

Her tone was lighthearted, but Pierre could tell something was wrong. Out of courtesy, he insisted. Michelle began to refuse again, but I went over to her, with my back to Pierre, took her hands, and asked her to come with us. She bowed her head and her red hair tumbled over her shoulders. When she spoke, her breath palpitated in her unadorned throat.

"I want us to stay here. You have things to say to me."

"I can say them later."

"I have things to say to you."

"We need to get some fresh air, love. We need to forget it all for a little while."

"Forget it all," Michelle repeated.

I told her I loved her. I told her we'd come back and keep talking. Look at the afternoon, I said. The sun's not shining, but there's lots of light, and I want you to come with us.

Michelle ended up accepting, and while we put on thick wool socks, sitting on the coach-house steps, she told me she was confident. For a moment, it seemed like she really believed it. She turned on the light in the little room and a moth flew outside. She got two pairs of boots out and looked for our jackets while I prepared the Browning and the ammunition. On the gravel courtyard, Pierre was playing with the dogs. He already had his rifle slung over his shoulder.

"It's difficult," said Michelle. "I suppose that's normal. These things have to be difficult."

"We'll try," I said.

"I know, I'm the one who wants to try. But I don't know if it can work. Be honest: you don't believe a word of what we talked about."

It was true. I'd imagined the moment of separation so

many times that I was now able to vary the details or the settings as if I were planning a film. Sometimes it would happen at night, after a fierce argument; other times, I'd leave before dawn, like a coward or a thief, aware I could no longer bear Michelle's sadness or the burden of her tears. Now I was assailed by the certainty that it would all happen sooner than expected. At any moment we'd look each other in the eye and understand there was no longer any solution. That's what I was expecting: a blow, painless and sharp. Then, as difficult as the moment might be, we'd each start over again on our own. And it would all, undoubtedly, be best for both of us.

THE PATH WAS COVERED in fresh mud. I felt the same pleasure as always, the pleasure of setting out from an open space where the stone buildings of Modave were visible, and advancing bit by bit, without changing paths, into the oilseed fields, through those crops of tall stems and yellow flowers where I used to get lost as a boy. Going hunting in the afternoons was different. Mornings meant large groups of old hunters, unavoidable rituals, solemnity. In the afternoons, it wasn't like that. One went out hunting to breathe the mountain air and to feel the silence and the solitude and the coolness in the trees. Pierre walked in front of us. The dogs ran several meters ahead, stopped to wait for us, then bounded ahead again. Michelle looked beautiful. Her hair changed hue against the corduroy collar of her jacket. The sky was a single cloud the color of smoke, smooth and uniform. Behind Michelle, almost at shoulder height, the stalks of the crop formed an even wall beside the path. A string of black ducks flew overhead, but too high.

"What did you bring?" asked Pierre.

I showed him the barrel of my rifle. The ducks were beyond our range.

"Doesn't matter. It's going to be a good day," said Pierre. "If it's like this here, imagine what we can find in the woods."

Pierre was superstitious. He wore the same socks every time he went hunting, and believed the first moments of a day determined what the rest would hold. The dogs loved him. They trotted along at his side, not mine. I said so to Michelle, and she smiled.

For about ten minutes we walked in silence. The landscape around us changed, and after we'd passed the Morés' place, we crossed the field toward the woods. Pierre split off from us.

"Where's he going?" said Michelle.

"He's going around the woods. He'll go in from the other side, to scare the animals."

"Toward us?"

"Toward us," I said.

"I want us to talk," said Michelle.

"Well, let's talk now," I said jokingly. "When we go in the woods, we'll have to keep quiet."

"I feel strange. I'm cold."

"In the woods it's not so cold, you'll see. There's no wind."

"Are we going to break up?"

I didn't answer. The furrows of damp earth required concentration: a hunter could break an ankle if he wasn't careful where he stepped.

"It's true it'd be better," said Michelle. "It's true we're hurting each other. But I'd like to know what you think. I don't know what you're thinking. I'd like to hear what you have to say."

Fortunately, we arrived at the woods at that moment, so I held a finger to my mouth to hush Michelle. I leaned close to her face, so close that her red hair tickled my lips, and spoke very softly. From here on in, total silence. Don't speak, step carefully, breathe in whispers. A boar can hear us from many meters away. If there are deer, the snap of a twig can scare them off.

The tracks of an abandoned railway line were covered in moss that sparkled with frost and raindrops from a recent shower. A false floor of fallen leaves covered the grass, and the leaves were wet and soft and opaque and golden, and Michelle liked stepping on them. I held her hand and we began to walk between the rails. The oaks and beech trees filtered out the wind. The air was dense and humid, the light filtered through the bare branches. There in the woods there was no noise. The world was green and gray and brown, there were no shadows, and nothing was moving. I think Michelle was happy.

I pointed to the spot where we'd wait, the place where the hill started down toward an open field. From there, kneeling on the damp earth and feeling its coolness, we overlooked the place the prey would run across, frightened by Pierre from the other side of the woods. I loaded my rifle. It was something Michelle had never seen me do. I tugged a piece of bark off an oak tree and gave it to her to sniff. Michelle inhaled deeply and a bit of dirt stuck to her cheek. She didn't feel it, because the cold air had numbed her skin, and I wiped it off with one finger in a movement that was very similar to a caress. I motioned to her to kneel down in front of me, so she could get a better view down the slope of the hill and the fallen tree trunks that had been caught up in the undergrowth. She liked the idea and crawled on her hands and knees without worrying about getting dirty. This, I didn't know why, made me feel sad. Seeing her like that, moved by the shapes and colors that moved me, her eyes open wide like a little girl, made me regret what hadn't yet happened. When had we failed at this? What words would which of us use to close off the possibilities? I thought back to the time when I'd fallen in love with Michelle. When I met her, she was a distracted and slightly brusque woman who was taking English courses at the University of Liège, but her only interest was in drawing letters to adorn the openings of books like *Le Morte d'Arthur* and *Lancelot du Lac*. This contradiction was emblematic of her way of going through life. On her T-shirts there was often a caricature whose outline, when it was cold, stood out from the pressure of her nipples. She used to ask me to pose for her, and she'd draw deformed figures in which my cheeks were like red peppers and my black hair, as in the Mandrake comic strips, appeared tinted with streaks of navy blue. At that time I loved her and everything was simple, clear, as evident as this uneasy reality, which would conclude with solitude, a necessary solitude but one requiring a sacrifice, a ghost sleeping between us like a small child. Realizing then that everything declines, that nothing lasts, made me think that living on my own would be less difficult. That's how I was feeling, midway between sad and resigned, when we heard three shouts from Pierre. I looked at my watch. We'd been kneeling on the ground and the moss for half an hour.

Michelle turned and looked at me with her big eyes, asking me wordlessly what that meant.

"That he's reached the end of the run," I said out loud.

"The run?"

"He's run out of woods, Michelle. And not a single animal came out."

"So? We're going now?"

"We're going now."

"What a shame. It's so nice here, all so fresh."

"We didn't come to look at the landscape. We came to hunt," I said. "And we haven't even seen a rabbit."

WE FOUND PIERRE sitting beside the path, playing with the dogs. Isis was biting the sleeve of his jacket and Pierre was letting her. Othello was lying in a puddle to cool off, and his fur looked like a vagabond's blanket. Pierre stood up when he saw us coming. He told Michelle he was sorry, that not all days were like this, that it was a shame she'd been bored.

"But I wasn't bored," said Michelle. "Just the opposite."

"Ah," said Pierre. "Well, well. But next time will be better, I'm sure."

"I was just fine," said Michelle. "We had a nice time. I don't know about you guys, but I was breathing and I felt alive."

Michelle was walking with her shoulders raised, looking at the sky.

"I want a nice hot coffee," she said. "Come back and have some *tarte au riz*, Pierre."

She didn't want us to talk anymore or, at least, she'd voluntarily forgotten. I was grateful. Michelle felt light. With a bit of luck, it might be contagious.

"A nice big piece, some good coffee, get the fire lit," said Michelle. "What time is it? I can't believe there's still light."

"It's starting to get dark now," I said.

"That doesn't matter. There've been years when you can't see a thing by this time."

"I'm glad you came."

"Me too, love. I feel different now."

Suddenly, Pierre moved his arm in the air. He pointed at the planted field next to Michelle. I raised my rifle. Pierre snapped his fingers and the dogs understood.

Isis and Othello broke through the curtain of yellow flowers, barking. Then a pheasant took flight and I aimed and the sight traced its movements and the barrel followed its desperate flapping and when the shot rang out the pheasant's left wing was broken in midair, paralyzed, and I knew I'd hit it, then the body turned sideways and fell slowly, like the silhouette of an airplane, into the yellow flowers. The dogs were barking, but I heard the thud of the body hitting the ground. It all happened in a couple of seconds.

"I'll get it!" said Pierre, and ran toward where the body had fallen. "I'll bring it!"

"Come on," I said to Michelle.

I jumped over the shoulder of hardened earth between the path and the field and began to look for the pheasant. My boots got tangled in the stalks and sunk into the damp soil.

"Where are the dogs?"

"Isis!" shouted Pierre. "Isis! *Cherche!*"

"Do you see it? Pierre? Can you see it?"

I'd only wounded it. A pheasant is very fast on the ground. The flowers reached our waists, and it was impossible to find, unless we stumbled across it or it tired itself out, or its heart had stopped and it was already dead. I tried to look for traces of blood, but all I could see was the earth under my feet. It was like wading across a muddy river.

"He's going to get away," said Pierre. "Isis! *Cherche-le, merde!*"

The barrel of the gun was like a machete and I used it to move the stalks out of my way. The damp soil at my feet came suddenly into view and then disappeared again. But the pheasant was nowhere to be seen. We couldn't hear it, the dogs hadn't found it, and they leaped among the flowers and kept looking.

"Shit," said Pierre. "Shit, we've lost him."

"We haven't lost him," I said. "Othello! Find him!"

"Useless dogs. We've lost him."

We stopped running. Pierre and I looked like bronze busts on a yellow carpet. We started to walk back to the path. Pierre called the dogs again.

Michelle was waiting for us.

"You didn't come," I said. "Looking for it is the best part."

"I didn't want to," said Michelle.

"We lost him. It was a magnificent pheasant and we lost him."

"You're not hearing me. I didn't want to."

"What's the matter?"

"The shot hurt my ears."

I tried to stroke her hair. She dodged my hand.

"It hurts. I can feel the shot inside."

Michelle touched her head. Her hand was pale in the cold air. The gunshot had upset her.

"Here inside."

PIERRE LIVED NEAR the Rue des Trois Maisons, in Modave, so he turned off before we did on the way home. Michelle did not reiterate her invitation to drink coffee by the fireside. We took a few minutes to get away because the dogs refused to follow us when we called.

"I can't wait to get back," said Michelle.

"I don't know if there's any wood."

"What?"

"We've had the fire burning all week. If there's no wood, I can go get some."

"Ah," Michelle said. "No, it's not that. I feel dirty. I want to get out of these dirty clothes. I can't stand wearing dirty clothes."

It was getting dark when we reached the house. Michelle went in, turned on the courtyard light, and left her boots on the step. I picked them up and carried them into the coach house. In the coatroom, I brushed them off on the doormat, cleaned the caked mud off the soles with an old screwdriver, unloaded the rifle, and looked on the shelf for the .20-caliber box, because in hunting season I accumulated bullets of all kinds in the pockets of my jackets, and sometimes had to go from pocket to pocket and get my ammunition back in order. Then Michelle came in.

"The truth is I think we could have found it," she said.

It took me a moment to understand what she meant.

"But we looked," I said. "You saw us."

"I don't think you tried very hard. Have you no pity? The bird is suffering right now. You should have found him and killed him."

"The dogs looked. They're good dogs, Michelle. We did everything we could."

"You left it to suffer."

"What's the matter?"

"You're cruel. You must not be quite right in the head."

She went quiet, waiting for me to say something. She was standing in the doorway, and the room's yellow light hit her from the side and made her features stand out on her face. I felt worn-out. I had to look at the rifle that I'd already put back in the rack to make sure it wasn't still hanging from my shoulder.

"And what do you want?" I said. "You want me to go look for it?"

"Don't be sarcastic."

"No, I'm going to go," I said. "See you later."

"But it won't do any good now."

"It doesn't matter. I think I should, Michelle. Give us a chance to take some deep breaths, count to ten, all those magazine recommendations. . . . We just can't stand each other anymore, can we? Who would have thought it would jump out at us like this."

I saw her hand move to her mouth and press her lips together between two fingers. It was her gesture of control, her secret mechanism to not start crying.

"Fine," she said. "Tell me one thing."

"What?"

"Are you coming back?"

There was fear in her question.

"If you're not coming back, tell me. On the whole, I like a bit of advance warning for things like this."

"Of course I'm coming back," I said without looking at her. "What a stupid question."

I walked out into the courtyard and the cold air hit me in the face. It was night and it was autumn, and the temperature had dropped drastically. Isis barked when she heard me open the gate.

THE FIELDS ALONG THE ROAD were the color of the night sky. Streetlights, in this part of the Ardennes, were almost nonexistent, and only the hay bales wrapped in white plastic broke through the darkness, big and round like balloons of light. I drove through Hamoir and crossed the whole village without seeing any lights on. The Maison du Pêcheur was closed, but Luca's old Ford slumbered on its gravel forecourt. Luca was a friend to all the local hunters; he would buy the day's catch and paid well, and in the evenings the little lounge to the left of the bar would fill up with men dressed in gray and green, their boots still caked with mud, shouting and arguing about the day's results. But tonight they'd already gone. I knocked a couple of times on the oak door; the place was dark, and the yellow lights of the level crossing reflected back at me from the steamed-up windows. I thought that any bright, warm place was as good as the next, I thought of the *friterie* on Rue Saint-Roch, and it felt good to get back in the pickup and close the door and be out of the wind again. Inside, it smelled of damp clothes, but also of Michelle's perfume. The road shone under the yellow lights until I got to the edge of town. The radio forecast fog.

The *friterie* on Saint-Roch was a mobile home permanently parked on the corner of Rue Saint-Roch and Route de Marches. It was white and dirty, and inside they served sausages and hamburgers and *frites* and *gaufres* with hazelnut cream that I'd never tried despite having passed through there a thousand times. As I walked up the wooden steps, I ran into a group of German tourists, and thought they must have come to see the races at Spa. The premises smelled of bleach. I found a two-hundred-franc note among the bullets and shells still in my pocket. At the table in the corner, beneath a collection of old bottles, two men were drinking beer. Above the window frame were disposable cups and a thick glass key ring. The men's checked shirts were identical except for the color; it was as if one of them had bought both shirts, or as if someone else had chosen them. Apart from those two and the woman in a ridiculous red uniform, who was making the cash-register buttons chime as if her life depended on the volume of that ringing, there was nobody else in the place. I ordered the same as those men, *frites* and a beer. I chose a table I could see my truck from. The men didn't look at me.

The older one had a harelip and his sparse mustache made it even more noticeable; the fingernails of the younger one were covered in a black film. I didn't get as far as figuring out what kind of work they did but thought they would probably be taking a transport truck to Brussels or even to Paris, because they didn't seem to be in a hurry to leave. The whole scene gave an impression of false calm, because the woman had stopped manipulating the cash-register keys and now her hands were busy organizing the things on the counter. There was something vaguely vulnerable about her, and it amused me to realize she was frightened. But then I thought it was perhaps legitimate that a small young woman—she wasn't actually that small, but her fragility created that illusion—should be frightened, working alone and late in a fast-food place on the side of a dark road. I went up to the counter.

"What did you have?" said the woman.

I pointed to the remnants on the table. A cardboard plate with a bit of mustard on it and a can of Judas.

The woman wrote large numbers on a paper napkin. She pronounced a sum and I gave her some money. When she was handing me my change, a five-franc coin fell on the sheets of grease-stained wrapping on the counter.

"Don't be scared. They're truck drivers, they won't hurt you."

The woman looked at me, as if checking to make sure she didn't know me. Then she looked toward the back, avoiding my gaze. In the irises of her eyes, I saw the brief reflection of the illuminated window. Suddenly I felt uncomfortable, intrusive, unwanted.

"Sorry," I said. "I thought—"

"It irritates me that people can tell," said the woman. "Everybody knows what I'm thinking, it's terrible. It's as if my face is a neon sign."

"You wouldn't be great at poker."

"No," she said. "You're not the first to tell me that. Do you think they've noticed as well?"

The truck drivers were drinking unhurriedly. Nothing

ever happens in the Ardennes; but all men are unpredictable, and anyone can be a rapist or a murderer. I felt that my presence was the only thing that gave the woman any peace of mind, and that power seemed immense and valuable. Or the woman's peace of mind was valuable, and the possibility of her being afraid again hateful.

"I can stay for a while, if you want."

"Oh, no," she said with a sudden pride. "None of that. I can look after myself."

"I can stay until they leave."

"And how can I be sure?"

"Sure of what?"

I thought I saw her smile.

"That you're not the one who's going to attack me."

The woman behind the counter smoothed a pleat in her red uniform, rubbed her index finger over her full, penciled eyebrows. Her skin was ash-colored, paler on her cheeks and broad forehead, darker under her eyes. On her right nostril sparkled a tiny diamond, worn with elegance like a family crest; when a wisp of hair fell over her face, she pushed it back under the red taffeta ribbon holding her hair flat.

"I don't know," I said. "I guess you have no way of knowing."

She looked at me and smiled, but the fear had not evaporated from her face. Maybe it was a permanent feature, as

Michelle's red hair was for her, or the scar to the right of her belly button. When she was twelve, Michelle had had an appendectomy.

"Why don't you ask for a morning shift?"

"There are no shifts here. I work all day."

"Oh. You're the boss."

"The bosses live in Aywaille," she said.

She turned around and took the aluminum mesh basket out of the hot oil.

"Thank goodness it's time to close. I'm not in the mood to stay here tonight."

"I can give you a lift, if you want," I said. "As long as you don't live too far away, of course."

"Don't worry. I live right here."

"Here?"

"A couple of houses down the street. Very close by."

"Just as well," I said. "Is there a phone?"

The woman moved her hand in the air. I walked toward the back of the place. On an old pedestal table, in a little back room, was a black telephone with several automatic dialing keys. It wasn't a public phone: the woman was doing me a favor.

Michelle's voice sounded alert.

"I thought you'd be asleep."

"Where are you?"

"In Saint-Roch. I wanted to let you know."

"I want you to come back. I didn't mean to say what I said. This isn't going to end, is it?"

I'd heard that question a thousand times. In those moments I felt that Michelle, by forcing me to be optimistic, was also forcing me to lie. I reproached her in silence. I know you're going to leave. That's what was waiting for me: a woman who tells me she's leaving. I was glad not to be able to see her now, and that she couldn't see me. I felt hypocritical when I said:

"Of course not. We're going to see this through."

When I hung up, I stood by the little table for a few seconds. I'd wanted to hear Michelle's voice, but now the conversation was ringing in my head like a rising bruise after being punched. The silence of the place bothered me. I went back out into the restaurant and again the air filled with the smoke of burned oil. The men in the checked shirts had left. Without bothering anybody, without putting anybody in danger.

The woman had taken off her red uniform. She was wearing a long black skirt and a windbreaker for the cold. "I changed my mind," she said. Under the neon lights, the diamond in her nose looked like a drop of mercury.

"It's so cold out," she said. "Can you give me a lift?"

THE WOMAN LIVED up Rue Saint-Roch toward Rue sur-les-Houx, about five hundred meters from the *friterie*. I imagined her repeating the route every night, at this time or later, and in the image I conjured up, I don't know why, it was snowing. I didn't believe for a second that her name was Zoé, but I didn't tell her that. We pulled into a small cluster of three identical houses, with smooth mown lawns as if nobody had ever stepped on them. When I stopped the pickup, I saw a silhouette spying on us from the house opposite.

"Don't pay any attention," said Zoé. "That's Madame Videau. She's very old and very nosy."

In the redbrick walls, not a single light was visible.

"Nobody's waiting for you?"

But Zoé had already gotten out. I watched her walk toward the door, red like the door of a doll's house, with her hands clasped behind her back. She stopped as if gazing at the façade. She turned around and her mouth moved soundlessly. I rolled down the window on the passenger side.

"I asked if you'd like to have something to drink," she said.

I caught a whiff of Michelle's perfume from the back of the seat, where her red hair had rested. No more than twenty kilometers separated me from where she was sleeping, or not sleeping, alone and without me. I looked at the clock: it was still early. I'd never made love with a woman who had jewelry in her nose.

"Sure," I said. "I'm still freezing to death."

I followed her inside. The living room was an enormous exercise in mimesis: nothing in it proved that Zoé had any taste of her own, much less decorative fancies. There was barely room for the two floral-print sofas and glass table, on which sat a box of cigars and a paperback copy of *The Little Prince* in English. I looked for the room where things would happen that night. The hallway Zoé was walking back up, with a lacquered tray in her hands, led to two closed doors. Zoé put the tray down on the table. "I don't have any alcohol," she said in a slightly apologetic tone, as if she were embarrassed. I asked her if we could light a fire and she nodded. I pointed to the cigars, asked if I could have one, and Zoé stammered, she said of course, said I don't know where the matches are, sorry, I'm a terrible hostess. It was suddenly obvious they didn't belong to her. I left my cap on the back of the sofa and asked:

"Is the book his?"

Her eyes rested on the mantel of the fireplace.

"Is your husband away on a trip?"

"My husband died three years ago," said Zoé. "He was a test pilot for new planes."

She fell silent for a second. Then she added, as if this would rescue the balance of the conversation:

"But he didn't read that book, either. He wanted us to read it together to help me learn English, but he died before we did."

The revelation shocked me. Not so much what I'd heard, because cuckolding a dead Englishman didn't trouble me, but rather the color of those words, the melancholy, the unexpected innocence. I put the cigar back in the box. A bit of leaf came loose and fell onto the glass of the table.

"His name was Graham. His plane crashed just before he reached Dover."

"We don't have to do this, if you don't want to."

"Right in the English Channel, imagine. No survivors."

"I can leave right now and nothing will happen."

"The sea is icy cold there. I've been told there are sharks, but I think it's a lie."

"Listen. Maybe it would be better if we saw each other some other day."

"Stay there," she said. "Please don't leave."

She straightened up the box of cigars, which I'd moved, to restore the symmetry of the table. The tray troubled her, and she ended up putting it on the floor. Zoé moved around her house as if it were a museum, and I realized she tried at all costs to keep it as it had been when Graham was alive. But she kept talking.

"Have you ever met anyone like this before?"

"Like what?"

"A woman like me. A young woman whose husband has died."

I imagined the effort it was costing her to call herself a widow. I pronounced the word in my head. *Widow.* Its sound and the image of Zoé did not correspond to each other.

"No," I said. "Never."

"Ah. Well, now you see. We're an interesting race. The first days, you worry a little when the person doesn't arrive at the usual time. And then you remember, see? That's the first days, and it hurts. Later, you start waking up at night, very late or very early. You think someone's holding you, and then you start to cry and you don't know whether out of love or out of fear. That always happens. To everyone."

"It always happens like that?"

"I've read a lot. It's the same for everyone. Sometimes the stupidest thing occurs to me: I think if only I'd been prepared, everything would be easier now. But I wasn't prepared."

"You weren't prepared."

"No. How were we going to imagine?"

"What?"

"That we wouldn't have time. Why didn't anyone tell us how everything worked?"

I wanted to touch her. I felt that would help. Then she said:

"Can I ask you to spend the night with me? Just to stay here, not to do anything, I'm not asking for anything and I don't want anything more. Can I ask you that and for you to respect it?"

Her blouse was missing a button. I hadn't noticed before. Behind the material, her collarbone was rising and falling like that of a cornered animal.

"I'd need a blanket," I said. "It's horrible to sleep with your jacket on."

———————

I LOOKED AT MYSELF in the bathroom mirror. It was true that the pajamas fit me, and curiously, I didn't feel too out of place. I'd only asked for a blanket, but Zoé led me to the bedroom and opened a drawer with a geometric design etched into the wood.

"They were Graham's." She handed me a shirt and pair of pants the color of smoke. "I'm sure they'll fit, you're the same size. If you don't want to wear them, it doesn't matter. I'm just giving them to you so you can be more comfortable."

"I want to be more comfortable."

"Oh, good. Then you can change in the bathroom."

And again I saw her smile. But this time she bit the tip of her tongue, and I could almost recognize that texture and felt a breath of tea and fresh water. Absurdly, her smile became a sort of prize or offering.

Now, from outside I could hear minimal noises from Zoé, who moved around the house like a little mouse, collecting the drinks, rinsing the glasses in the sink. I heard her come into the bedroom, open and close a closet. She knocked three times on the bathroom door.

"Yes?"

"Don't come out. I'm changing."

"Okay. Let me know," I said.

I kept myself busy by snooping around the bathroom, the

details of someone else's bathroom. Since I was little, a locked door has always given me a sensation of absolute impunity. There was a cheap tape recorder in Zoé's bathroom, sitting on a small enameled glass shelf. Beside it, a disorderly pile of three cassettes without cases. All the labels said the same thing: RADIO MUSIC. I imagined this woman recording songs from a radio station without bothering to edit out the commercials, and listening to the recordings until she knew both sides of the tape by heart, and then repeating the whole operation. I had never looked at solitude so closely. It was as if at that instant someone revealed the rules of the game.

When I came out wearing the pajamas, smelling of wood and mothballs and dotted with flecks, Zoé was already waiting for me between the sheets. I was cold, the skin prickled on the back of my neck. I wasn't obliged to make conversation: my script only called for my staying in the bed until dawn, filling a form whose emptiness was painful for Zoé. But I wanted to know what Graham was like, put a face to that name, and Zoé took out a spiral notebook with black pages, opened it to the first one, and showed me a dark photograph. I recognized the bed where I was now lying, the lamp on the bedside table to my left that in the photo appeared beside a crystal glass and a pair of sunglasses barely visible in the shadowy image, and I thought that Graham must have had a headache that night and the water was to take a pill with, if indeed it was water, and the headache might have been due to the strong summer sun during some maneuvers. However, in the photo only Zoé appeared, seated in the lotus position on her pillow. Her body was the only luminous point in the frame. The rest were vague suggestions of objects or profiles that were lost entirely in the uniform black of the edges.

"Where is he?" I asked.

"Almost everywhere. We were studying photography, going together to a studio here in Ferrières."

I brought the paper close to my face. I examined it.

"He's here?"

"Yes, he's walking. If I look illuminated it's because he's standing beside me shining a light, first on one side of my face, then my body and knees. Then he walked around the bed and in front of the camera, and he lit me from the other side."

"He's walking past here. He's in front of the camera?"

"But we'd turned off all the lights. The room was in complete darkness. He was explaining what the teacher had explained to him. He was saying: "Now I'll open the diaphragm as wide as it goes, and take the photo over the course of fifteen minutes. You have to stay still the whole time, try not to blink.""

"Fifteen minutes," I said.

"In those conditions, the camera only captures what is very still and illuminated from up close. Nothing is shining on him and he's also moving. That's why he can't be seen."

Zoé passed her hand over the image, as if she were performing a magic trick.

"But he's there," she said. "Even though we can't see him."

Zoé put the notebook back in the drawer. "Can you hold me?" she asked, and I stretched out my arm and she took refuge in my embrace. Her head smelled slightly of sweat. I thought that she would be taking in the familiar scent of Graham's clothes. Before starting to feel sleepy, I heard her speak, almost to herself.

"When I feel very lonely, I turn off the lights. I pretend that this is the room in the photo and I am the one in the photo, and Graham is here running back and forth. There's nothing odd about my not being able to see him. It's just a question of optics."

I woke up shortly before first light. Zoé was sleeping with her back to me, breathing through her mouth and with her arms relaxed. As I was getting dressed, I thought *Saturday, November the first*, and then I thought *All Saints' Day* and then I thought of Michelle. I left the pajamas neatly folded beside the headboard of the bed. I left without saying good-bye, so as not to remind Zoé that she'd slept beside another man, to let her live for a few minutes more inside the spell she'd woven.

The house had been devoured by a bank of damp fog. The pickup's fan was on, and what the night before had been heating was now a blast of ice-cold air. I didn't turn on the radio. I wanted, without knowing why, to preserve the predawn silence, the gentle repose of the mountain, the pleasure of not seeing anyone in the sleeping streets: all that filled me with the sensation of testing out a new pair of eyes. In a short while, the men who had survived the night of the dead would begin to come out of their homes. All those who had worn disguises—as had I, who spent the night in a dead man's clothes—to survive this night, would soon be emerging, and all those who had bribed the spirits with offerings. I counted myself among them. I was alive, in spite of having been chased by souls of sinners trapped in animal bodies. Because I knew that the night that had just passed was the last of the old calendar, the moment when debts are paid, revenge is taken, and the dead are buried so their bodies will rest during the winter. But on this night, the curtain that separated this world from the other was torn: souls were freed from their captivity and some walked the earth, divesting men of their brief pleasures, sowing discord, broken hearts, and terrifying solitude among them.

It amused me to think of all that. It was Michelle who first told me about the superstitions of Halloween. She told me it was a shame that children here didn't dress up and go out and ask for candy. She told me about Celtic legends, drew their symbols, wrote out for me the names of some of their goblins. Pinch. Grogan. Jack-in-Irons.

Michelle, the woman who was still my wife. Who had been far from me for so long, too long.

———

WHEN I GOT HOME, the fog had not yet cleared. I opened the gate and the iron stuck to my fingers like dry ice. Before I got to the stone steps, I saw Michelle standing in front of me in underwear and a T-shirt, a paper tissue clutched in her right hand. Her eyes were the color of her hair and the tip of her nose looked irritated.

"Go inside," I said. "You're going to catch cold."

"You told me," she responded.

"Calm down, nothing happened."

"You told me you were coming back. I fell asleep, but I was waiting for you until half an hour ago. I was waiting for you, I fell asleep, you didn't come back."

I held her gently: her body was like a badly fired ceramic and was threatening to crack or fall to the floor and smash into pieces. She kept talking.

"But I don't want this to happen again. I don't want nights like this."

"Nobody wants nights like this," I said. "But we still have time."

"You wanted to leave. I know it. You don't have to lie to me."

"Come on, let's go upstairs."

"I've been crying all night. I'm tired."

"Yes, but you don't know how much I want to be with you."

We went upstairs. It was warm in the bedroom and it was

good to be back. I took off my clothes and lay down on the bedspread. Michelle lay down beside me. "You're exhausted," she murmured. "I can tell." A crow flew past the big window that overlooked the lake, and I asked Michelle to close the curtains. In that lake there were small trout. The day I asked Michelle to marry me, I remembered, I'd caught two. At that moment, two trout had seemed like a good sign.

"I wonder where the bird is," said Michelle. "I hope he's died, poor thing."

"Hope so," I said.

I thought later I'd go out to look for the pheasant, and that I'd like Michelle to come with me to look for it. I thought of proposing this to her, but she'd fallen asleep on my shoulder. I wanted to explain that we were going to be okay. I wanted to tell her that we'd made a lot of mistakes, and hurt each other a lot, but we didn't do any of it out of cruelty, but rather trying, maybe in mistaken ways, to suffer as little as possible. I surprised myself feeling that the most difficult part had just begun.

"Nobody wants nights like these," I said to Michelle, although she couldn't hear me. "We're not going to have to live alone."

With the tip of my thumb I wiped away a dribble of saliva at the corner of her mouth. She snuggled her head against my chest and I closed my eyes to listen better to the silence of the early hours, the way the murmur of the heating mingled with the sounds of the Ardennes just as Michelle's breathing began to mingle with mine.

WE LET THE MORNING go by without rushing it, and around midday I discovered there was no dry wood to light a fire with. I hadn't been able to at Zoé's house, either—Zoé, that already strange name, that distant night that belonged to her, not to me—and now the image and feeling of a crackling log fire turned into a sort of craving. But I didn't go out to Modave to get a bundle, because I didn't like the idea of being away from Michelle. Instead, I phoned Van Nijsten's shop, in Aywaille, and a woman asked me to wait, and while I did an electronic version of a Jacques Brel song played in my ear. Then the same woman told me that Van Nijsten wasn't there but someone would deliver my order in thirty minutes.

"Anything else?" asked the woman.

"She's asking if we want anything else," I said.

"Not for me," said Michelle.

Michelle had taken a long shower, and after her shower we'd made love slowly, having taken the time to unplug the telephone and turn the digital alarm clock around, and then she had dried her hair and put on a soft pearly lipstick. But what I remembered, after all that, was how I had sat on the floor to read while she was showering, leaned against the wall beside the bathroom door, and a sliver of wood from the frame had snagged the right sleeve of my pullover. I took the sweater off and fixed the bunched thread by pulling on it with my teeth, while I heard the water pouring over Michelle and let myself be calmed by it, because the running water meant that Michelle was there, and hearing her shower, worrying about a sweater that she had given me, I felt comfortable and simple and satisfied, and I thought that must be happiness.

When the doorbell rang, Michelle was about to say something.

"Go ahead, get the delivery," she said then.

I opened the door to a man with a bare head. His scalp was so cleanly shaved the glass of the door was reflected on it. The man put the wood down beside the poker and left the bill on the mantel, took the money, and left, all without saying a word. I knelt down in front of the fireplace.

"Okay, now we're ready," I said, rubbing my hands. "You were going to tell me something."

"Have you got matches?"

I said yes, I had matches and several editions of *La chasse aujourd'hui* to burn. I made a bed of paper twists on the grate. When I was arranging the kindling and logs, I heard Michelle.

"On Thursday I was at my parents' house. I'm going to spend some time with them."

I stayed still, as if paralyzed. Maybe I believed that, if I pretended not to have been listening, the words would fall into oblivion.

Michelle went on talking. She said she no longer had any hopes for this, and that love seemed to her a distant emotion, something that no longer had anything to do with us. It hurt her to speak of love that way, like a dog that had run away in the middle of the night, while she was alone. But that was the truth. She had glimpsed it last week—on Tuesday, after eating alone in front of three bulletins from Euronews—and she'd talked to her mother and her mother had told her to think it over carefully. She did as she was told: she didn't want to give in to her first impulse; she preferred to give us a few more days, give life a chance to straighten out its course.

"Now I've thought about it, while I was in the shower. And that hasn't happened, nothing has straightened out. I want to be alone. I don't want us to go on hurting each other."

"Is that why you took so long?"

"What?"

"Showering. That's why you were so long in the shower?"

"I don't know, love. I don't think that changes anything."

"You had it all worked out," I accused her. "You've known for a long time, and you made us carry on with this farce."

I imagined her naked, letting the hot water hit her face, or leaning on the wall of the shower with her eyes closed and the cascade of her hair stuck to her shoulders. How had she decided? Had she thought of me, of a history of my mistakes? Had she recalled any happy moments, perhaps ones that I didn't even remember, to then confirm how much everything had changed? I could think back, too, but the only thing that came into my head would be the coolness of the air this morning, when I got home and Michelle was waiting for me. It was cold air, but it didn't have the harshness of winter; it was air that was pleasant to breathe, and I had breathed it avidly and had felt that every lungful was cleansing my body. At that moment, the world was as simple as bread fresh out of the oven. The spirits of the night of the dead had gone back into hiding, and Michelle was waiting for me.

"Are you sure? Is there nothing we can do?"

Michelle covered her face with her hands.

"Almost all my clothes are at my parents' house. I took them when I went to visit, just in case."

"And if someone helps us? If we were to see someone?"

"I'm ready," said Michelle. "I can leave this afternoon, if you want. So we don't drag this out."

I felt sorry for both of us. Out of fear of feeling faint, I kept my eyes fixed on the bare match between my fingers. I realized I'd stopped understanding, that I'd lost control of something: the immediate course of my own life, Michelle's emotions, or, simply, the idea of a splendid renovation I usually glimpsed like a prophecy when I thought of us splitting up. And the most uncomfortable aspect was to feel that some semblance of truth was about to be conceded to me and I hadn't managed to know what it was about. I closed my eyes to listen to the voice that perhaps wanted to speak to me, to show me something about this moment. But nobody spoke in my head. Maybe this moment didn't have any meaning, after all. Maybe pain and loss had meaning only in religion or in fables. Maybe it was futile to look for meaning in the shapeless vertigo that now, for the first time, filled me from within.

"And now what are we going to do?" I said.

"I don't know," said Michelle. "We're going to be fine, I imagine."

THAT AFTERNOON, after I dropped Michelle off at the station in Aywaille, after waiting with her for the orange train that would take her to Liège and seeing her get into the car and put the yellow knapsack I once brought her from Paris in the luggage rack, after asking her to call me when she arrived and hearing her say *I promise, I'll call as soon as I get in,* after saying good-bye and walking out of the station along with the rest of the relatives and friends who'd been saying good-bye to their relatives and friends, after all that, I decided to pass through Saint-Roch before going home. But the trailer was closed, and I peered in the window and the kitchen was not working and the oil was not boiling. It seemed strange to me that a place like that would close on Saturdays. I looked at it from the outside: things are bigger in daylight. I waited awhile, then went to look for Zoé at her house. I didn't find her there, either, but I found something better: there was a note hanging on the gray mailbox, stuck with insulation tape, that Zoé had left for someone. I read: *I won't be long, attendez-moi.* And trying to imagine who would be waiting for Zoé, trying to investigate the plural request and the circumstances of the day, I thought that Zoé wasn't so alone after all, if she had people willing to wait for her on a Saturday at five o'clock in the afternoon. I realized then that the note was written on an English postcard, and I thought Graham would have brought it back from some trip, and from the caption under the image I found out it was a bronze plaque in Liverpool, perhaps near the port, and that those English words, *courage and compassion joined*, were an homage to the musicians who'd died in the shipwreck of the *Titanic*. I put the postcard back in its place and made sure it was well stuck, pressed the insulation tape firmly, because it would be terrible if the wind blew it away and Zoé's friends left without waiting for her due to the breezes that usually blow in the Ardennes. I drove out of the neighborhood before Zoé returned, and on my way I imagined her going out to get the wine she hadn't been able to offer me the night before, or buying some pastry at L'Épi d'Or for her guests. Of course, it was also possible the note was not directed at any friend, but at strangers who were coming to fix her hot-water heater or dishwasher or maybe leave her a bundle of firewood in anticipation of winter. That was also possible and I knew it. But I preferred to hold on to the other idea.

The Lodger

THE NIGHT BEFORE, at around nine, Xavier Moré had arrived on foot at the Lemoines' house. He suddenly appeared in the kitchen, filling the doorway, looking like an old scrounger. His skin was as dry and rough as blotting paper, and the wisps of white hair across the top of his head looked like paint peeling off a clay wall.

"I've come to get my car," he said.

Georges and Charlotte looked at each other.

"Why don't you come in and have a hot drink?" she said. "We're just finishing dinner."

"I don't want anything. I just want my car."

Several months earlier, Jean Moré, Xavier's only son, had asked Georges if he'd keep his father's old Porsche in the barn. "He's still drinking a lot," he'd said. "I'd rather chauffeur him around than see something happen to him on the highway." The strategy worked out well: Xavier began to get used to being a passenger, even seeming to forget he'd ever sat behind a steering wheel. Meanwhile, the Porsche slept in Georges's barn, surrounded by bags of manure and rusty shovels.

"The car's here, but we don't have the keys," said Georges. "Your son has them."

"That's a lie," said Xavier. "The keys are here, too. I want it. It's mine and I want to drive it."

Georges listened closely: there were no traces of alcohol in Xavier's voice. He couldn't remember the last time anyone had arrived on foot. It hadn't happened since wartime, when they were young enough to walk the five kilometers between their houses without breathing any heavier. More than once they'd gone as far as the border by bicycle, unconcerned about the risk of running into German soldiers, to buy potatoes at lower prices. But now they were old men, and old men don't walk alone, at night, braving the autumn cold of the Ardennes. Georges took Xavier by the arm, led him to the table like a blind man, and Xavier accepted a glass of port: no matter that he'd suffered an attack of gout a couple of weeks earlier that had forced Jean to hire a nurse from the Rocourt hospital. Georges wanted to say: Don't worry, think of tomorrow. Tomorrow everything will have changed, one goes hunting and forgets the bad things.

"I don't really know why I came," said Xavier.

"You wanted to see us," said Charlotte.

"Well, yes. But it wasn't urgent."

"I have an idea. Why don't you stay overnight? You can't go back at this hour."

"We could call a taxi," said Georges. "There's a car service in Aywaille—"

Charlotte cut him off. Her blue eyes reproached him for something.

"We don't need any taxis. The guest room is made up."

"This is stupid," said Xavier. "My Porsche is sitting in your barn and I want to take it. What has my son told you, might I ask? I'm fine. Do you think I'm drunk?"

"We'll call Jean," said Georges.

Xavier lifted his arm and the wine in his glass was illuminated with a yellow light. He threw the glass down on the wooden floor, hard. But the glass didn't smash: its stem snapped off with a quiet sound, and the port spilled out, forming a long puddle.

"Merde," said Xavier.

He fell back in his chair, his head in his hands. "Just as well. The doctor said I wasn't allowed any." He didn't look at Charlotte, but said:

"I wanted to talk to you."

"Well, talk to her," said Georges.

"It was nothing. I was feeling lonely, it happens to us all."

"All of us," said Charlotte. "But that's why there's—"

"Not to you two, of course. You're the happy family, the little house on the prairie."

"What's that supposed to mean?" said Georges.

"Nothing, nothing. Don't get paranoid."

Then there was a knock at the door. Xavier smiled, and in his smile there was a bitterness Georges had never seen.

"There's my son, flesh of my flesh, blood of my blood. It's touching. Everyone worries so much, they notice I'm not home and go out looking for me."

BUT ALL THAT had been the night before. Today, Georges didn't want to worry about bitter thoughts. Charlotte took his hand and he felt the roughness of her skin. He adored that roughness, and hearing his wife's smoker's voice, and stroking her gray hair, calmed him. Xavier chose his life without anyone forcing him to do anything. The past was far behind them, everyone made their own selves. That was terrible, but it was true.

He poured himself some coffee and thought he could add a few drops of cognac without harming his aim. The mountain cold had stayed in his hands, and as he lifted the warm coffeepot his fingers thawed out. It was almost eight in the morning and the room was beginning to fill up with people and voices. Hunters crossed the paved courtyard with long strides; through the window Georges watched them arrive.

The rubber soles of their waterproof boots barely dented the silence. Some of them left the back doors of their four-by-fours open, and the dogs barked from inside their cages when a tortoiseshell cat ran past toward the lake.

Georges knew the routine by heart. Jean Moré, the host, was welcoming the hunters, and at his side was Catherine. Tradition forbade a hunter's wife serving as a beater, but they didn't concern themselves about that. Sitting at the dining room table, standing in the faint light coming in the window, or trying to warm up in front of the fireplace were the rest of the beaters. They had fluorescent jackets flung over their shoulders and hunting horns hanging around their necks like medallions. It was the same team as ever, except for the presence of a novice toward whom Jean was feigning tolerance.

"Gentlemen." Jean raised his voice. "I'll ask you to finish up your drinks and come outside. It's time to get started. I don't want the morning to slip away before we've all done what we've come here to do."

"Well," said Georges. "We're getting under way now."

"Go and kill lots of boars," said Charlotte. "And bring them back to me, and I'll cook them for you just the way you like them, and we won't share them with anybody."

Georges kissed her on the forehead.

"I'll go, kill 'em, and come back," he said. "Like in the movie."

There wasn't yet complete daylight in the yard. The sky

was still overcast. In the inner courtyard, figures cast no shadows. On the paved surface, boots surrounded Jean with a murmur of rubber. The hunters wore green, but no green was the same as the next. Their jackets were thick fleece, adorned with yellow edges like fine epaulets and deer embroidered on the lapels, with buttons like coins on the sleeves and deep pockets in which nothing jangled, no keys, no matches, because those were garments for the hunting season, and no daily or habitual objects, nothing betraying domestic life, would ever be forgotten in their pockets.

"The circle, gentlemen," said Jean.

The hunters surrounded him. Jean gave out the orders of the hunt speaking with his trumpet in one hand and a lit cigar in the other. Jean was one of the most respected hunters in the Ardennes, as his father had been, and Georges still felt moved at seeing the son of his best friend acting as *maître de chasse*.

"I have little to tell you, gentlemen, because you all know the rules. No shotguns, rifles only. Do not fire into the encirclement or toward rocks. The first boar is off-limits, as are females, roe deer, and stags."

He kept quiet for a few seconds, as if looking for a way to round off his speech. After a moment, he let his cigar get soaked in the drizzle, took two steps toward the barbecue, and threw it in with the firewood.

"That's it," he said. "Good luck, and good hunting."

The group dispersed on the other side of the gate. Each hunter seemed to have arranged beforehand which four-by-four he'd be riding in. The doors opened, the cars began to spew brightly colored supplies—red and purple plastic cylinders that looked like pieces from a children's board game—green arms checked rifles, opened and closed portable stools, and the beaters pulled on their orange vests.

Xavier was leaning against Georges's four-by-four. He held a black umbrella and a folding stool, the leather of which had been mended several times. Georges approached him without speaking. He patted him affectionately on the back and a cloud of dust came off his coat.

"How are you?"

"Fine. How else would I be?"

It was as if they hadn't seen each other the night before. Georges decided to play along. He helped Xavier stow his rifle behind the backseat, with his own guns. Like several of the hunters, Georges couldn't help bringing his old Browning shotgun on the hunt, even though he knew full well that its use would be forbidden. Balanced among the guns was a big mushroom he'd picked on the way there that fit perfectly, and wouldn't get too knocked around along the way.

"Hope your dog doesn't eat it," said Georges.

Stalky, Xavier's dog, was a golden retriever, old like his owner and tired from hunting with him for more than twelve years. An illness had damaged his sense of balance some time ago, and he walked with his head tilted to one side as if he were looking at a crooked picture.

"My dog doesn't eat mushrooms," said Moré.

"I know," said Georges. "I was joking."

"Yeah. Well, don't make ridiculous jokes."

They went across the Route de Modave and headed toward Aywaille, and only stopped at the north edge of the forest long enough for the beaters, sheathed in their fluorescent vests like neon scarecrows, to get out with the dogs and each take up their positions. The varied barking of the beasts and a mélange of their names filled the air. Stalky barked, too. "You're not getting out yet," said Xavier. "You're staying with me." From the other side of the grounds, a narrow track that would only allow the vehicles to proceed single file—one car behind the next, bumper to bumper—led to a field that the hunters would cross on foot on their way to their positions. The barbed wire along the edges of the track was almost grazing the doors of the four-by-fours.

"Why are they stopping?" said Xavier.

"Here comes your son." Georges leaned out the window. "What's going on, Jean? Why are they getting out?"

"This is where we're going to leave the cars, Monsieur Lemoine," said Jean Moré, who was coming along assigning positions. "Park as close as possible to the one in front, to leave space."

"Give me the keys," said Xavier.

"I have things to get out of the back, too," said Georges, and then asked Jean: "Where's my stand?"

"In front of the woods." Jean pointed.

"Give me the keys," said Xavier.

"Yes, yes, don't be impatient," said Georges, and took the keys out of the ignition and handed them to Xavier without looking at him. "And your father? Where should he go?"

"On the corner of this side." Jean's hand moved through the air, indicating the precise angle the trees established. "If there are any boars, these are magnificent positions."

"They're useless positions," said Xavier.

"That's not true, Papa."

"If you were assigned that spot, you'd be offended."

It was true, but Georges kept quiet. Being patronized this way had stopped mattering to him quite a while ago. With his dry hand he reached for an apple in the glove compartment and stuck it in his right pocket; he felt the warm contact of the fleece and his arthritis let up for an instant. Xavier, who did wear gloves, criticized him for his stubborn refusal to cover his hands on these freezing mornings. By the time Georges got out, Xavier had already unloaded all the gear they needed. Stalky was beside him, howling. Georges checked his door. Before letting go of it, he asked:

"Have you got the keys?"

"Don't worry, you can close up. I've put them safely away."

"Okay. But don't let them jangle."

"Don't worry," said Xavier, "I won't be moving much. You're a lucky man."

"Nonsense, our positions are as good as each other. They're spots for old hunters. But we are old hunters."

"I was talking about Charlotte," said Xavier.

His eyes had reddened and his skin was turning pale: it was almost possible to see the blood retreating from his forehead and cheeks. Two or three times in the last few years, always after too much wine, Xavier had come out with some brusque comments about Charlotte. This was the first time he'd touched on the subject while sober. Georges, however, confronted the matter with the false tolerance of someone talking to a drunk.

"No hard feelings," he said.

"Of course not. She chose you. She stayed with you. What hard feelings could there be? Don't be a hypocrite."

"All that's past. The only thing—"

"All right, all right," said Xavier. "Spare me the philosophizing, I beg you."

He can't stand seeing us, thought Georges, *he can't stand seeing what we've attained.* They went their separate ways. In front of the southern edge of the forest was a pasture where three Limousin cows were grazing. Georges looked to the right and to the left: Xavier, hunched over, was heading to his position with Stalky trotting eagerly at his side, and the complicity or harmony that had developed between the dog and his owner over the years was plain to see; on the side nearest the road, the crowd of younger hunters broke the line of the horizon. The vision of the armed silhouettes reminded Georges of those images of men disembarking in Normandy during the war. He walked patiently toward the spot he'd been assigned. He was, for the first time since the day began, truly alone. He was grateful. He stopped, inhaled the cold air, and all the mountain smells, manure and pine, rain and damp moss, washed over him like a wave. Every once in a while, an isolated engine broke the silence, and the only noise that Georges heard, while he settled down, was the sound of the joints of his portable stool as he unfolded it over the dead leaves. Soon, as he loaded his rifle and shotgun, he heard the echo of the metals colliding and, when he finally sat down, putting his gun across his lap and leaning his rifle against an oak tree, the uneven chorus of horns that announced the beginning of the hunt. Suddenly, the image of a Flaubert book and a train ticket to Nancy came to mind.

THE DAY GEORGES TURNED FIFTY was also Jean Moré's initiation to the hunt, Jean having killed his first boar that very morning. Charlotte organized a gathering at home for friends of the family and some fellow hunters. The boar's head rested on its side on the lawn, beside the stump of an oak tree. The

LOVERS ON ALL SAINTS' DAY

hunters shouted, let's see him wearing the head, put it on, and Georges eventually lifted the head and set it on Jean's head like a hat. Not much blood spilled, but enough to give Jean's black hair the look of a cow's placenta, and the baptism was complete. Georges would later think that eating with hands dirty with boar's blood wouldn't have been so bad. But, at that moment, it hadn't occurred to him to act any other way. He went inside through the kitchen door and his eyes took a couple of seconds to adjust to the darkness. He found Charlotte sitting on the floor beside the gas stove, surrounded by pheasant feathers. She had her apron on; she was not crying, but she was panting as if she'd been running. On top of the plastic table-cloth was the pheasant they'd be eating later, its throat slit and innards now cleaned out. On the other side of the bird, the Flaubert book: a blue hardback with gold lettering.

"I was going to leave you," said Charlotte.

She seemed convinced that the world would not be transformed after those words, or that she'd be able to fight against the transformation. Like a puzzle, everything fit together in Georges's mind. But it was too late (a thousand little signs proved to him) for reproach or jealousy, for confrontation or a scene.

"He gave you that book?"

"Yes. With the train tickets."

"To where?"

"France."

Georges looked out the window. Xavier and Jean were playing with the boar's head. The most obvious strategy for the adulterer was to show up at social gatherings where his lover would be. That way he gave the impression of not having anything to hide and, therefore, that nothing was actually going on.

"I thought I was pregnant," said Charlotte. "We were going to live in Nancy until the baby was born."

Georges looked at her chestnut hair and the vertex on which the button of her blouse joined the line of her breasts. Having a child with Xavier in another country was a way of beginning a new life. Later Charlotte and Xavier would have married. Everything would have gone back to normal, and they might even have returned to Belgium. But Charlotte wasn't pregnant. She'd chosen not to run away; she didn't need a new life.

"I'm staying," she said. "I'm staying with you."

"Are you sure?"

"You don't know how much I've suffered. I don't want any more of this. I want us to go back to being ourselves."

"But we haven't stopped being ourselves, Charlotte. You've lied very well. You have an admirable talent."

"No sarcasm, please."

"Also, you're not young. This is no time to be having babies."

"Let me stay."

"How long has it been going on?"

"I don't know," said Charlotte. "Three, four months."

"Exactly."

"I don't know, dear."

"Of course you know. That book is an anniversary gift, I'll bet you anything. *Madame Bovary*. He's not what you might call subtle, our friend Xavier."

They did not embrace. They did not kiss, not even like friends. But their marriage was safe, even if just for this moment. The next step would be to work at it, work tenaciously. Georges loved her, and that certainty should be enough for him to go back with Charlotte, for that complicated return to the body of a woman he'd never left. That Charlotte was not young, at forty-five, was false, but that didn't prevent them from feeling the excitement of the surprise of realizing they'd stay together, that they had their whole lives ahead of them.

TO FRIGHTEN THE PREY, to force them to leave the woods and expose themselves to the hunters' sight, each beater had developed a particular and private voice that Georges, over time, had begun to be able to distinguish. He made an effort, a sort of personal challenge, to discern them in the air. That *ooooooo* with hands clapping was from Guillaume Respin; Frédéric Fontaine shook the bushes with a polished stick and shouted *ah-ah-ah-eeeee*. Catherine had decided, quite a while ago, to do without onomatopoeia.

"Get a move on, brutes!" she shouted. *"Foutez le camp!"*

But no animal escaped down this side. With a bit of luck, the hunters on the other side would trap at least one boar. Georges looked up, but the pigeons were flying too high: it would be arrogance for a man whose aim was not as sure as it used to be to attempt such a shot. Nevertheless, he pointed his rifle at the gray sky and looked through the telescopic lens, dusty and smudged with fingerprints: years ago he would have tried, he thought calmly, his finger caressing the trigger. He lowered the gun and listened to the beaters; the commotion of branches breaking under their feet didn't drown out that other commotion of their threats. It was possible to follow those movements among the trees, because the boundary of the woods was clearly established and the way the wind played with the sounds intensified the voices as soon as the beaters came around the western corner.

Then three shots rang out.

"Tiens," Georges said to no one. "Someone's had some luck."

He tried to relive the sound of the shots, and smiled as he guessed someone had fired a shotgun and was going to be admonished by Jean. He imagined the prey, made bets with himself: a young boar, an out-of-season deer, a banal rabbit that had made someone react too quickly? He was attentive to the rest of the noises. The beaters were covering the second flank of the woods and the dogs barked as if to cut through the cold.

A fourth shot rang out.

Georges inhaled deeply, because ever since he was a little boy the smell of gunpowder in his nostrils, in case by chance the wind was blowing in his direction strongly enough after a nearby shot, had fascinated him. He couldn't smell anything this time. Instead, he was surprised to hear the three horn blasts signaling the end of the hunt.

Why were they stopping already? Didn't they still have a good stretch to cover? He didn't react yet, waiting for confirmation. A hunter shouted from somewhere:

"Pap, pap, pap."

Georges didn't hide a grimace of disappointment. That was the sign: the hunt had been called off early. What had gone wrong?

"Pap, pap, pap," he shouted in turn.

Swearing, the hunters began to show themselves throughout the forest. They no longer walked calmly as they had earlier in the morning, but hurried like boys; they wanted to get back to the cars as fast as possible and find out which beater had sounded the trumpet three times before having gone all the way through the woods and settle that innocuous blame, and then, finally, carry on to the next place. Georges did the same. He didn't stop to sniff the air. He wasn't paying attention to mushrooms or chestnuts fallen among the grass. He didn't even allow himself the basic curiosity of who had shot what. His gaze was fixed on the line of cars of which his, being the last to arrive, was now the first. He was pleased about that: he'd leave before the rest, avoid hearing the disputes and reproaches. When he was getting to the end (now the beginning) of the convoy, he saw Jean arriving almost at a run, his face disfigured with rage.

His wife was following him. Five meters or so behind them the group's novice was walking. His lank reddish hair had fallen across his face and he had recent acne scars on his chin. Georges knew Jean's words referred to him, not to the others: Respin and Cambronne hadn't even appeared yet, and the rest of the beaters were too far behind to even hear him.

"Idiot! He's an incompetent idiot! We've completely wasted the woods, shit. How incompetent can someone be. But by God he won't be coming out with us again. If it's up to me, he won't ever be with us again."

"It wasn't him, dear," said Catherine. "I was with him, I swear it was someone else."

"I had to learn the hard way. But one thing's for sure, this is the last time a beginner gets his first chance on my hunt."

"But it was someone else," said Catherine.

"Everyone back to their vehicles," shouted Jean. Dark

looks from one or more of the hunters reminded him that he was speaking to older men who deserved respect. His tone calmed down then; but in his throat remained the suppressed fury of a spoiled little boy.

"I beg your pardon, gentlemen. Someone brought this station to an end ahead of time, and we've missed out on some good opportunities."

"Where's your father?" said Georges.

"I propose we simply forget this matter and proceed to the next stop."

"Jean," said Georges.

"Yes sir." Jean turned impatiently.

"Where is your father?"

Jean looked around at all those present. He looked toward the field, looked at the grazing cattle, looked over the barbed wire.

"Has anyone seen my father?"

The heads moved from one side to another, like at a tennis match.

"Where's he got to?" said Jean, lowering his voice.

He leaned on one of the posts holding up the barbed wire. A notice stapled onto the wood said: PROCEED WITH CAUTION. HUNTING SEASON. NOVEMBER 1986.

"Well, it doesn't matter," he said at last. "He'll catch up. To your cars, gentlemen."

"But we can't leave," said Georges.

"Why's that?"

"Your father has my car keys. He kept them for some reason."

The line of cars was stuck. There was no way to move a single one of the four-by-fours, not even a meter, without Georges moving his first. And his was locked and the hunter who wasn't there had the keys.

Jean's hands flew to his head. He looked at the beaters. He was about to order them to go and look for his father and bring him there as quickly as possible, when Respin and Cambronne emerged beside the wire fence.

"Monsieur Moré," said Respin, "can you come with us?"

"You blew the horn? Which one of you was it?"

There was no answer.

"Really, my friends, men with your years of experience . . ."

But the beaters didn't say anything.

Jean felt for a cigar, felt for his lighter. Georges, although from a distance, managed to see that his thumb was clumsy as it sparked the lighter, and that the tall flame trembled in the hand that trembled. Jean's hand had trembled. Georges gathered up the sympathy he was unable to feel at that moment and offered:

"Go with them. I'll come with you, I'm right behind you."

Jean's eyes shone. His feet had turned to stone and did not want to move.

"Please, Monsieur Moré," said Cambronne, "come with us."

Jean and Georges followed them in the direction of the forest, trying to keep up. Georges felt in his chest and thighs the effort that pace was costing him. From behind he could see the two beaters, the line of their shoulders that rose and fell in a terrible cadence, the color rising in their cheeks. Still from behind he saw them stop and look at each other (not with a look of someone questioning or conversing, but with a vacant expression that only wants to avoid the present urgency), and then look at Jean, who arrived alongside them. In the center of that incomplete picture, framed by three pairs of rubber boots—one gray, another tobacco-brown and filthy, the third pair green and tied up with fine laces over long woolen socks—was Stalky, shot several times. A wide gash in his side stained his coat; some fur stuck to the viscous flesh. His still-palpitating guts steamed in the cold air, and the blood was an intense red against the green of the grass. Two steps from the animal, fallen in the undergrowth, Xavier's lifeless body came into view.

Georges saw Jean lose his self-control. He saw him throw himself on his father's body and open his shirt without really knowing what he was doing, as if the impulse to do something, anything, was moving his hands with memories of imagery picked up from films. The chest was pale, and the hairs that outlined a snowy forest formed, as they reached the neck, a tangle of stiff, dry clots. Jean spat on his hands and tried to clean his father's shoulders off with the saliva on his palms. Then he began to pummel the body. "Get up, Papa," he said. "The hunt's not over, it's just that the novice blew the horn too early." When Georges put a hand under his arm to lift, Jean had a tuft of wool between his fingers. Just like when he was a child, thought Georges, just like when the three of them went fishing and Georges would be shocked at how much patience Xavier had with that spoiled little boy who was always wanting piggyback rides and digging things out of his father's belly button with his baby finger.

"Everyone left so soon," said Catherine quietly. "I never thought I'd feel so lonely in my own house."

Georges looked around: indeed, the hunters had slipped away without a word, little by little, like the tide going out. At our age, he thought, nobody likes to think of someone else's death. He was wearing his leather shoes, and the feeling on his feet was agreeable, fresh and firmer, because in old age his ankles had started to ache after wearing rubber boots. In the reading chair that no one in this house used for reading, Charlotte was sitting in an oblivious position, as if she'd forgotten she wasn't alone. She crossed her legs, and her drill pants rode up above her ankle, revealing porous white skin and a sock whose elastic no longer worked very well. There was some wisdom in her dark drill pants and man's shirt and her face with no makeup. She'd always refused to have children, and now that he was old, Georges had convinced himself that this characteristic formed part of the same description in which he would have included the masculine cut of her shirt. And now Georges was looking at her. *You're thinking about him.* He realized his forehead was heating up and took off his overcoat. Under his arms were dark sweat stains. But earlier, when he'd had to embrace Jean to distract him, he'd behaved with an unfamiliar calm. When he'd held Jean's head between his hands, to draw his attention away from the fissure in his father's skin and the vision of the destroyed muscles and the appearance of a thick, white tendon like a worm in the burned flesh, at that moment, Georges was another person. The people from the Modave commune took forty minutes to get there. The ambulance, with its siren and flashing lights turned off, five minutes more. In all that time Georges did not move. His feet were planted on the ground like a bullfighter. Jean wanted to be cradled in his arms. The woman from the commune began to ask questions, and Catherine answered them as if she were taking an oral exam. Only when the body was ready to be transported did Georges begin to feel a headache from the deferred tension. Catherine approached Jean. "They're asking if you want anything, or if they can take him." Jean turned on her.

"How stupid you can be sometimes," he said.

And he climbed into the ambulance.

Now, Catherine walked between the swinging kitchen door and the table where the spout of the coffeepot had stopped steaming. She poured herself a glass of port and went to sit under the floor lamp, closer to Charlotte than to Georges. She looked pale, and her voice was laden with sadness.

"What did they do with Stalky?" she asked.

"Respin," said Georges, "and some others. They buried him right there, in the forest. They'd already seen some vultures circling."

"You should have gone with him, dear," said Charlotte.

"With whom?"

"Jean," said Charlotte.

"No, he shouldn't," said Catherine. "There are lots of people with him, people who know about these procedures. I need company, too, Madame Lemoine. I think I'm more bewildered than my husband."

She took a sip from her glass. An imprint of her lip remained on the edge, because Catherine used a moisturizing balm before going out hunting to keep from getting chapped lips. Then they heard the noise of a car's engine, and the sound of gravel displaced by tires. Catherine stood slowly, went out to the porch, and returned and sat down. "It wasn't him," she said. It was Respin, coming back.

"What will it be like now? Madame, what was it like when your father died?"

"You'd better ask him," she said, gesturing toward Georges. "I barely remember."

Georges kept his face blank. He preferred to avoid the subject.

"He was with me," said Charlotte. "It was the beginning of the war. I saw it all from the window. My father ran, it was stupid to run when we hadn't done anything, the soldiers fired and he slipped and when he fell to the ground some crows were startled."

"How old were you?"

"Seventeen."

They looked at the pale rectangle of the window. Respin walked past in the direction of the stables, his hands holding up the lapels of his coat, his hair blown about by the wind. "He can't keep still," said Catherine. "When he's nervous, he'll invent any excuse not to sit down. There are times when Jean can't stand it." The novice followed him with a shovel over his shoulder. Georges thought he saw a trace of blood on the edge of the aluminum, but then he thought that shovel had been used to bury the dead dog, and maybe knowing that detail was manipulating his imagination. Away from the hunt, an animal's death always shakes us up, thought Georges, perhaps because it seems not to have any justification.

"One of the crows had a blue ribbon tied to its leg," said Charlotte. "I guess it must have escaped from somewhere."

"They weren't getting along," said Catherine. "Now it's going to stay like that. That's what I don't like."

Catherine had changed into a more comfortable outfit—now she was wearing a green sweater with a roe deer embroidered across the left-hand side of the chest—and, after unplugging the phone from the front hall and plugging it in behind the reading chair, brought a chair from the dining room, placed it beside Charlotte, and began to make calls with an address book open on her lap. The pages were thick embossed paper, and the panels of her small and full address book looked hand-drawn. While she spoke, Catherine ran her index finger down the black lines. Georges listened to her dictate the details of a notice for *Le Wallon*. Xavier Moré. M-O-R-E. Comblain-la-Tour, 1917. "He just died," she said, and hearing the deliberate imprecision of her phrase seemed to surprise her. Charlotte, meanwhile, distracted herself with the illustrations that appeared in the notebook, on the facing pages of the directory. She lit a cigarette. Georges watched her inhale deeply; the straight line of the smoke, bathed in yellow light, was like the trail of one of those planes Georges hated, because they brought back memories of the war, and flew over the Ardennes frequently these days, toward the NATO military base.

Catherine covered the mouthpiece with her hand.

"They're maps of places that don't exist," she said. "Chinese, Armenian, things like that."

"Maps of paradise," said Charlotte.

"Yes. Some of them. But they're not all religious, look. This is a map of the center of the earth."

"Are they not helping you?"

"They asked me to hold. This is the first time I've done this. You two don't have to stay until Jean arrives, Monsieur Lemoine. You look tired."

"I am a bit."

"We can stay a little longer," said Charlotte. "It's no trouble, is it, dear? Besides, I want to see more of these maps, they're fascinating."

"I don't know. It's almost dark."

"It's barely five," said Charlotte.

"Seriously? And night's almost fallen, how incredible."

"They've got this little tune playing," said Catherine. "Funeral parlors are so funny . . ."

Charlotte put a hand on the book. Her skin was dry and blue veins mingled with wrinkles. Beneath her long, marmoreal fingers were the phone numbers for the letter H and a sort of aerial view (as might have been produced by one of the MiGs that flew over them) of the Labyrinth with Happiness in the Center. ENGLAND, 1941, was printed in the margin.

"Xavier gave it to you, didn't he?"

"To both of us. Before we were married. One day he showed up with it as a present, just like that, for no special reason."

"No reason," Charlotte repeated.

"I mean, it wasn't Christmas, or either of our birthdays."

"Yes," said Charlotte. "I knew what you meant."

Then someone came back on the line, and Catherine held the receiver between her shoulder and head to take down the details of the ceremony. *Tomorrow, 2 pm. Burial 3 pm.* Charlotte took the pencil from her hand, crossed out *tomorrow* and wrote *Friday.*

"For later," she said. "One likes to remember what day it was."

She smiled a sad smile and added:

"Who knows why."

Catherine looked at her. Then she lowered her head.

"Is it going to be really horrible? For Jean, I mean."

"Make love," said Charlotte. "That helps, I think."

IT WAS COMPLETELY DARK when Georges pulled up to the junction of the road to Hamoir and the road to Marches. He turned right where Catherine's pickup truck once ran out of gas, several years ago, and Georges and Charlotte tossed a coin to see which of them had to go collect her. The twenty-franc coin had landed with the king faceup, so Georges had to put on his white dressing gown and siphon some fuel out of the smallest tractor with a piece of hose, sensing at each suck the imminent taste of gasoline and feeling sick from the vapors. Now—it seemed implausible to him—that ingenuous memory didn't end with early-morning laughter, with Charlotte's refusal to kiss him or even get close to him because his breath stank of gasoline, but in a question: Had they spoken in his absence? That night, while he was rescuing Catherine, had Charlotte phoned Xavier? Georges feared that the past was beginning to transform. He slowed down as they passed the gypsies' place, a mobile home embedded on the edge of the access road for so long that the lawn had devoured the tires and struts. On the aluminum steps leading to the little door slept a white rabbit, luminous in the night and puffed up with cold.

The house was getting to the stage when it seemed to be shrinking, because fewer rooms got used with the passing years, until some were opened only to dust them. It wasn't a spacious place, but they'd been able to build two stories and an attic in spite of the restrictions in force at the time. The front hall smelled of leather and furniture polish. As they went inside, Charlotte and Georges knew that falling asleep would be impossible. That fixed and invariable routine a couple of their age gets into was in their case one of fascinating symmetry: Georges took off his shoes and put on his slippers while Charlotte got the coffeepot and filter ready for morning; Georges went up to their bedroom while Charlotte took her arthritis medication, in the kitchen and almost behind his back, as they both maintained the fiction that she wasn't old enough to need it yet. But that night, none of that happened: they walked into the dining room listening to the wooden floorboards creaking under their steps, and while Georges sat down in his green velvet chair, Charlotte dug out the Stéphane Grappelli record. It was Xavier's favorite. After the concert in Liège in 1969, Georges had gone up to Grappelli and asked for an autograph. "For Xavier Moré," he'd said. Grappelli had signed the cover with a black felt marker.

She let the needle down onto the vinyl. The music sounded distant, as if coming from the other side of a curtain. Charlotte sat on the other side of the fireplace and switched on the radiator. Seeing her so distracted, in that effort to maintain her serenity, in that dispute with her own affections and with twenty-year-old ghosts, made Georges feel strange, almost superfluous in his own house.

"Do you know why he did it?" he said.

"As if you care," answered Charlotte.

Georges stood up and offered her a cigarette. Charlotte was not surprised that he'd guessed her wish. The lighter's flame whispered as it burned the paper around the tobacco.

"He was my friend, too, you know," said Georges. "Or rather, he was my friend *most of all*."

"That address book was going to be a gift for me," said Charlotte. "Or rather, he did give it to me."

Georges had imagined. He chose not to say so.

"But you didn't accept it."

"I couldn't. But it's so pretty."

"That was after you'd decided to end it."

Georges's phrases walked a fine line between statement and query. As he spoke, he looked at the bellows and old newspapers; he stared at the wood in the fireplace although it wasn't lit. He knew he was irritated with Charlotte, and the effect seemed obscurely agreeable or necessary.

"A long time later. Like four years. We'd drifted apart, there wasn't any risk. Nothing would have happened if I accepted. But I didn't accept it."

Georges made no comment. He listened to her describe the paper Xavier had used to wrap the gift, a page from the newspaper. But not just any page, it was the front page of *Le Wallon* from March 11, 1963, the date of the last time they'd made love. It was here, said Charlotte, it was in our guest room, Xavier was my guest for a couple of hours and then he left, before you got back from Liège, because he knew he wouldn't be able to look you in the eye that afternoon. Charlotte had torn the paper angrily and thrown the notebook, with all her might, and it had ended up in the hydrangeas and they'd had to ask Nadia, the youngest daughter of the gypsies, to climb into the shrub to retrieve it. Xavier behaved very stupidly afterward. He gave Nadia a hundred-franc note and told her not to tell anyone about what had happened, and she, with hydrangea petals in her hair, took it without knowing what it was all about. "Why, dear?" said Charlotte. "Why bribe an eight-year-old who's done nothing but look for a book in the flowers? You'll scoff, but at that moment Xavier struck me as a faint-hearted coward." Georges did not scoff. He just listened.

"But it was a lovely little address book," said Charlotte.

"Useless, though," said Georges. "Maps of places that don't exist."

She pretended not to have heard.

"Later, I asked him if I could borrow it to photocopy one of the maps. Xavier had already given it to Catherine, but he took it for an hour and photocopied all the maps at the paper shop in Aywaille, the one beside Riga. I saved one of those photocopies, just one, the one I liked best. I still have it, dear. If you want I'll show it to you."

THE ENGINE GAVE three false starts before finally firing up properly. As far back as he could remember, driving a tractor relaxed him, but this was the first time he'd done it at night. Luckily there was no wind, because the cold would have been unbearable; the night was dark, the clouds invisible, the threat of rain persistent. The field where the neighbors' cows occasionally grazed was less than one hectare; the grass grew during the spring and part of the summer, and Georges waited anxiously for the moment he could climb on his tractor to mow it. It was an old machine, a Ford 5000, but it still worked well; the Gallignani baler it towed collected the hay with its forks and bundled it into cubic-meter bales, which it tied up with a rough cord, so later the youngsters, Jean and his friends and sometimes Catherine, could go around the field picking them up with a pitchfork and taking them to the barn to store until they were sold. This year, the summer was long; at the end of September there was still hay to cut, and tonight, the last Sunday Georges had climbed on his tractor to cut and bale hay seemed recent to him. The land was covered in dry yellow stubble, and had taken on that look of an old dog who's lost too much fur. Georges flipped a switch; above his head, three white lights came on, the yellow of the loose hay brightened, and shadows appeared behind the wooden posts. It was as if Georges was wearing a gigantic miner's helmet. The serenity of the night—the crickets rubbing their legs, the short howling of wind in the trees—was soon drowned out by the private racket of the engine. Under the dome of the night sky, in that clearing of light that seemed to come from a reflector hanging from the heavens, Georges felt vulnerable.

What he'd seen in Charlotte's eyes was not nostalgia: it was nothing immediate, nothing present; it was barely a memory of an infatuation. But it bothered him, perhaps because of what that memory might illuminate. In the pocket of his shirt, folded in four, was the map of the Islands of Pleasure. Charlotte had handed him the page, saying:

"The original is from an eighteenth-century watercolor. It's from Rajasthan."

And she'd quickly added:

"That's in India."

Georges was shocked by so much precision. The conferring of a date and a geographical location didn't prove anything, didn't make the map more credible; pretending to give reasons for which those islands might have been able to exist although in reality they didn't exist, the date and place achieved, for Georges, the opposite effect. But it would be different, of course, if another person were the origin of that page. Twenty years earlier, it was his wife's lover who'd handed her what she'd just handed to him. Against his chest, against his left nipple, the page burned; on his tongue, the word *Pleasure* had a bitter taste, like an unripe blackberry. That was probably not the only thing his wife had sought from Xavier, but he felt that resolving this doubt would console him.

The night smelled of dry grass despite the imminence of winter, which kills fragrance. Georges looked in the direction of the house. An eye of yellow light floated in the air, the tiny bathroom window. He knew what that meant: the door between the bedroom and bathroom was open. Charlotte was reading, or pretending to read, in bed and getting ready to sleep. But she wouldn't sleep tonight. At that moment, the tractor turned the corner of the pasture and Georges had his back to the light. The noise of the engine and the pinion and the roller isolated him, and behind the tractor he was leaving a corridor of a trail. Any hunter, he thought, could track and shoot him. He was lost in these absurd ruminations, thinking of how he could outwit the hunters coming after him, when the tractor turned to face the yellow window again, and in it was a silhouette. Charlotte's arms moved in the air, as if she were a shipwrecked woman who had glimpsed a rescue ship. Although he could not hear her, although focusing on the expression on her backlit face was impossible, Georges understood there was some news about Xavier. He left the tractor by the wire fence and walked toward the garden. On the sandstone patio, the chairs leaning up against the table suggested a restaurant that had just closed. Only when he was a few meters from the wall did he look up. Charlotte was a bodiless face disfigured by perspective, a statue on a church's domed ceiling.

"He's ready," she said. "We can go to the wake."

"You want to go?"

"Of course. I don't know. I hadn't considered not going. I feel bad, dear."

Georges looked down. Dry leaves were piling up beside the stone wall. He tried to exaggerate an impatient face so it would be visible in the half-light.

"And why you? What do you have to do with this?"

"You told me yourself that he talked about me on the way

to the hunt. He's been in a bad way for a long time, everybody told us. And it's as if what happened before banned us from worrying, you know?"

"No," said Georges. "What you're saying is absurd."

"He was our friend. And we haven't allowed ourselves to take him seriously, to lend him a hand. As if what happened before would come back, what a couple of idiots. Jean wants to talk to me, but I'm not going alone. Will you come with me?"

Georges did not cushion the harshness of his words. He felt contemptible and, without knowing why, also felt that he didn't deserve Charlotte. But that didn't stop him from saying what he was going to say.

"No. It's late. I'm tired and we'll have more than enough tomorrow."

Charlotte looked distressed. She spoke to him of the man who had wanted to escape this life, of the terrible confirmation that it was another life he would have liked to live and hadn't. Charlotte accepted that it was stupid, but in the past few years she had wondered what fault any of this was of hers; she had asked herself so often that now she couldn't help devoting all her attention to him: to try to accompany Xavier, even if only in spirit. Georges turned away as if to cut off his wife's words, because the mention of the spirit invoked for him, through some sort of piercing contradiction or terrible irony, the map of the Islands of Pleasure. On the lawn a rectangle of a more lively green was projected. Georges felt something fuzzy rising in his throat. He held his breath, and the nausea descended. He spoke to the silhouette's shadow.

"I'm going to be on the tractor for a while longer."

"I'm not going to go alone, dear. Won't you come with me?"

"No," he said. "It's your affair."

INSTEAD OF WALKING toward the orange shape of the tractor, he went around the house by the shed side and found, in the middle of the rough carpet of stable sawdust, Xavier's Porsche. For a moment, he wanted to sit inside it, but then the idea struck him as macabre. He leaned on the boot; the darkness was total. "Do you know what that means?" Charlotte had said to him. "Regretting now, at the age of seventy, the life one's chosen?" Of course, she'd said, it was hard for him to see all that: for him things had come out well, like for a poker player. A few years or months or days ago, even just yesterday, Georges would have said: This is what all past life is, the results of an ongoing strategy.

Now he wasn't so sure. But he had a hunch: the past would become imagining Xavier wearing his father's hunting jacket, a Frenchman who'd belonged to the *louveterie* and devoted his life to hunting wolves. Because that was a man, the clothes of those who'd gone before, and Xavier's were heroic clothes:

imagining him like that, romantically dressed up as a gentle-man of bygone days, could justify Charlotte's feeling attracted to him. But that tranquillity was artificial. Meanwhile, neither they nor anybody else could guess what had gone through Xavier's mind. Maybe it was absurd to think he'd killed himself over her, but everything in Charlotte's words seemed to suggest that. Now, it seemed obvious to Georges that only her sense of decency had prevented his wife from confessing that certainty. One doesn't reach such decisions by chance, that was true. But to think of such a long-ago cause . . . Did that really happen? Did men really kill themselves for love, and for long-past love affairs? What surprised him most was how Xavier's image began to change: he could no longer remember him as he was, those memories were already contaminated by his suicide. Georges admired the courage: not just of putting the barrel of a gun beneath one's face (just one traditional barrel; Xavier had not succumbed to the fashion for double-barreled shotguns), but seeing himself reflected, a second be-fore, in the death of a dog, and carrying on with the process of one's own death. It was incredible what frustrated love could do to a man. It could track him, the way dogs tracked the trail of the scent of prey (a wolf, for example), and hold him at bay. Georges, too, standing on the sawdust-covered floor, was a man at bay. He imagined Jean's phone call, the questions he would have asked Charlotte, that woman his father had loved.

Georges hated him: he hated him for involving his wife in all that. Then he retched again, and this time, without kneeling, Georges threw up watery bile smelling of wine and stale bread.

WHEN HE WENT BACK to the house, it was after eleven, and Charlotte, perhaps, would be asleep. Georges preferred to stay downstairs. A long time had passed since the last time he hadn't said good night to his wife—both beneath the covers, he overcome by weariness and she trying to read a couple more pages of some Montherlant novel—in the way routine prescribed. He imagined Charlotte was still dressed. Ready to go out, he thought, ready to go and see Xavier no matter how late.

He knew he loved her. He had always loved her, even when he found out about the deception. Now those episodes came back as if fresh, with that terrible attribute the past has of never passing, of staying here, and keeping us company. How could he have prevented it? How comfortable the future was, that future people so feared. Of course, they ignored how difficult the pain of the past was and the memory of that pain, because it was like clothes that have fallen in the hay in summer and keep scratching your neck and back all day long.

The previous night, after Xavier had left, Georges had

spent a couple of lazy hours cleaning his Browning, using silicone to repair a frayed strap, brushing the buttons on his hunting jacket. The implements hadn't been put away, and were still there, looking at him as if they'd warned him that today would be special and it would be better to stay home, that he should have made up some excuse to not go out boar hunting. He looked for the biscuit tin that he'd used to store ammunition as long as he could remember and took it into the kitchen. He put the kettle on, and the air smelled of gas and then burned match. While he was waiting, Georges began to organize the cartridges and bullets that got mixed up over time or just stayed there, on the windowsill and in the cutlery drawer, making the reality that no children lived in this house unmistakable. When he had all the 8x57s in a single pile, the kettle began to fret on the stove. Georges put a lemon tea bag in a thick glass, striped from use, and let two sugar cubes dissolve in the boiling water. With the biscuit tin in one hand and the glass of tea in the other, he went to sit beside the telephone. He took out the map of the Islands of Pleasure; for the first time he looked at it closely. Water flowed around a circle, and in the water two fish swam, one coming and one going, one trying endlessly to catch up to the other, but it was impossible to tell from the drawing which one was chasing and which escaping its pursuer. Georges turned the photocopy over and wrote on the back in pencil:

Charlotte Lemoine
Xavier Moré
Georges Lemoine (me)

Charlotte
Georges
Xavier (him)

To have lost her forever
Never to have been with her

He heard dogs barking, far away and distorted by the echo. Their house seemed different at night, and this silence, through which he usually slept, now stimulated him, made him tense and alert, aware of the whole world. He saw his reflection in the windowpane, translucent like a negative; he saw the shadow of the guns in their rack, like billiard cues, steady and disciplined. Perhaps overwhelmed by detail, in a mental atmosphere too similar to that of an opium addict, Georges did not pick up the phone at the first ring—he might have confused it with the barking, or he might not have heard it—and when he did, the black receiver fell asleep in his hand. Jean's voice called from the other end of the line, serious, electronic, disconsolate.

"*Allô? Allô?* Madame Lemoine, are you there? Madame, I need to know, I need to speak with you. You're the only one who might know."

Georges realized that revealing his presence would be like surrendering. Accepting that Charlotte formed part of that small tragedy, that she'd had power over the life of a man who was not her husband, would be to discover that he and his wife had not lived alone all these years, that there had always been a specter between them. Then he also realized that all those precautions were futile. It was naive or ingenuous to believe that the past was capable of burying its dead. From this night on, Moré would appropriate part of the house: he would be a permanent lodger, someone Georges would see by just turning his head while smoking a cigar or brushing his teeth, someone who would watch him and his wife sleep, standing next to their bed wrapped up in his father's green hunting jacket, until the end of time. Georges hung up the phone; he immediately unplugged it, yanking with such force that he broke the socket, leaving blue and red wires sticking out of the wall. He didn't stand up; his legs would not have done his bidding. He thought he was unable to go upstairs, to confront Charlotte's sadness, her silent tears, her likely guilt and perhaps her accusations. So he would stay faintheartedly downstairs, as he'd read about wolf hunters doing centuries ago in the Black Forest: parties of armed men who would allow night to overtake them among the trees, unable to return to the village without the body of the beast that had stolen their hens, dismembered their goats, and disturbed the slumber of their defenseless wives.

The Return

THIS IS WHAT HAPPENED when Madame Michaud got out
of prison. It happened at Les Houx, the Michaud family estate, and was not written up in a single Belgian newspaper.
The oldest episodes of the story occurred thirty-nine years
earlier, and were much commented on at the time, but now
there is probably nobody outside the family who remembers.
I'll tell the story as it was told to me.

Les Houx is a piece of land of about three hectares, acquired by Madame Michaud's great-grandfather toward the
end of 1860, when the country was young and, in the princi-
pality of Liège, property changed hands without any formali-
ties. Madame Michaud's grandfather grew up and lived his
whole life there, and so did her father. Madame Michaud and
her younger sister, Sara, were born and raised there, and both
lived there until, shortly after turning forty, in September
1960—a century had passed since the family took ownership
of the property, which was their emblem and their pride—
Madame Michaud was tried for the murder of Sara's fiancé.

She was found guilty of having fed the man rat poison used in the stables of Les Houx, and given a long prison sentence.

Madame Michaud's first name does not matter, but a clarification regarding her surname and civil status is in order. Michaud was her family name and the one on the sign at the entrance to the property: LES HOUX, PROPRIÉTÉ PRIVÉE. FAMILLE MICHAUD, 1860. Until that September, Madame Michaud was still *Mademoiselle* Michaud; she'd never been known to have a beau, and very few men visited her more than once, but no one ruled out the possibility that, even at forty, she might marry, for a piece of land like Les Houx was worth as much as the richest dowry and made either of the daughters a good catch. But when it emerged that Mademoiselle Michaud had been sentenced to forty-five years in prison, the *Madame* started to slip into people's conversations. There was in the title a mixture of respect and pity toward a person who could not now marry, and whom it was going to be impossible to carry on calling *Mademoiselle* while she grew old in prison. Madame Michaud was released six years before the end of her sentence, and the first thing she'd do, as everyone surely knew, was to visit the house at Les Houx.

Her love since childhood for the house and stables, the crops and woods, and even the bare fields that led out to the road, that boundless love, would be her undoing. Since she learned to walk, her favorite pastime was wandering through all the nooks and crannies of the house on her own. There was not a single corner of the immense building she did not know or would not have been able to find with her eyes closed. This might not seem such a great feat to those who don't know Les Houx. So I should say that the three-story house has two stairways that lead to the first floor (one from the kitchen and one from the front hall) and one more that goes directly to the attic. Its perimeter was regular, a perfect closed rectangle like a safe; but the design inside was not at all symmetrical, full of unpredictable niches and alcoves. There was a doorless room entered by sliding the false back of a wardrobe: their grandfather had hidden potatoes and cabbages there from his harvest to induce a rise in prices at the turn of the century, and their father had hidden a Jewish couple there during the war. Between the two events, the room had belonged to the girl. She was solitary by nature, and not even her sister knew where to look for her when it was time to sit down at the table or when she needed her for something. They'd know she'd been in the stables because she'd show up smelling of hay and manure; they'd know she'd spent the morning in the woods because her dresses would be torn by twigs and pinecones and completely ruined by sap from the trunks. When she grew up, her parents got worried: Mademoiselle Michaud saw doctors and the odd apprentice psychoanalyst, because it was incomprehensible to people that a nineteen-year-old girl would spend the whole day by herself instead of seeing her friends. No one understood why she could never be found in the same room of the spacious house; no one understood why she would squander her summers wandering around the three hectares like a cat marking her territory. The war broke out, and Mademoiselle Michaud gained sudden importance in the functioning of Les Houx: during the nightly bombing raids, when the whole country's electricity was cut so the planes could not locate their targets, she was the only one who could find things lost in the darkness, or cross the property from one end to the other if the horses needed feeding or a message needed to be taken to the steward. All this determined that, in 1949, when the girls' father died, their mother, who until then had taken little interest in such matters, entrusted the administration of the estate to the only person who could obtain satisfactory results; and Mademoiselle Michaud had the perfect excuse to forget or overlook the eagerness for marriage of the young men of Ferrières or Liège or even Louvain. In that state, which for her approached paradise, she was able to remain for several years. The house had never known—nor would it know—such splendor.

In 1958, Sara received a visit from Jan, a young man from Flanders whose surname no one could quite remember: neither her mother, due to lack of effort, nor her sister, due to self-absorption and indifference. Every Tuesday and every Saturday for two years he was seen arriving in a rosewood-colored Studebaker—which he parked in front of the house, where their father had parked since he bought his first car—

and leaving as soon as night began to fall. He rarely crossed paths with Mademoiselle Michaud in the house: as soon as she saw his car come through the gate, she disappeared. She found the man unpleasant from the first moment, and frankly repulsive from the summer Saturday when he arrived, not in the afternoon but before midday, with a crew of assistants carrying measuring sticks. Mademoiselle Michaud, from various corners of the property, watched them taking inventory, measuring the side that bordered the road, the area of the woods and the fields on which nobody had built anything, or ever thought of building anything. The following Saturday, further measurements were taken, following the same routine; and when she came inside, that night, Mademoiselle Michaud sat down facing her mother, who was calmly reading *The Red and the Black*. That trivial detail would stay with Mademoiselle Michaud forever, because at no point in the conversation did her mother close the book or even rest it in her lap to talk. With the book open in front of her, the leather spine facing the anxious daughter, her mother explained that Jan (and she made an attempt at pronouncing his surname) had asked for Sara's hand: she had found no reasons to turn him down and more than one to accept. Their father being dead, the decision fell to her and was not up for discussion. They would be married early the following spring. The first week of April seemed to everyone an excellent moment.

Mademoiselle Michaud began a slow study, which she

herself perhaps did not even notice and whose object was Sara's future husband. This might be called intuition, but also mistrust: the mistrust of a woman (because by then, Mademoiselle Michaud was a woman) who had never had much to do with human beings; whose friendly connections, in essence, had always been with the objects of the house, the beams of a ceiling and the carpets, the whitewash on the walls and the gravel of the courtyard or the wood of the sheds. Things and their arrangement in physical space were Mademoiselle Michaud's company; it was logical, then, that the presence of the betrothed and his measuring men should perturb her. She followed and spied on the couple; her knowledge of the terrain allowed her to go unnoticed. She saw without caring that, when they found themselves alone in the living room, they didn't just kiss, but his hand disappeared under her sweater, and hers among the folds of his tweed trousers. She saw, toward the end of August, that the fiancé began to arrive earlier, and he and Sara would take advantage of her mother's afternoon nap to hide in the room behind the wardrobe, from which the odd shy moan would escape. And at the beginning of September she saw Jan using the upstairs telephone to make a business call. He spoke of the time when half of all this would belong to him; he spoke of the necessity of putting so much unused land into production. The details he mentioned worked on Mademoiselle Michaud with the force of a catapult. Around that time she had to go to the border, where prices were lower, to purchase a large quantity of woodchips. Some merchant was able to supply the small grinder she was looking for. She returned home after dinner, and blindly emptied the contents of a little bag, a coarse, heavy powder, into the suitor's *pousse-café*. Jan did not survive the night.

Her mother, wisely, sent Sara to the house of one of her friends, in Aix-la-Chapelle. The trial was held swiftly, for the malice was obvious and the evidence overwhelming. A truck came to take Mademoiselle Michaud to the women's prison, near Charleroi. Her mother did not come out to say good-bye. I imagine the woman who until the age of forty had lived in the world of a little girl, and then had murdered someone, looking for the last time at the family estate. Two days later, Sara, still feeling sick, returned to Les Houx. She could not sleep, but that was the least of her woes. Before anyone noticed, she was bedridden with anorexia, a doctor had come to save her life, a therapy begun and punctually carried out; with time, her sadness became no more stubborn than any other sadness, and bit by bit her appetite returned. An accident occurred one day: her mother tried to force her to taste a *gâteau de macarons* she'd bought for her from André Destiné's patisserie, which had always been her favorite; Sara refused and in the face of her mother's insistence lost control, gesticulated too close to the table beside the glass door, and smashed a ceramic vase, which had belonged to her great-grandmother. Sara noticed the space on the table, the circle that shone like a moon where the vase had stood, unmoving, for so many years. It might be said that this moment marked the beginning of her recovery. She said that the dining room was now brighter; the next day she moved the table to a different spot; a week later, hired three workmen who, along with the steward, widened the frame of the glass door two meters on either side, and ended up replacing it with a large window from the parquet floor to the ceiling.

They never received any news of Madame Michaud—this was how the public now referred to her—and Madame Michaud had no news of them. People commented that it was as if she'd been sentenced to the harshest exile from the start and, in time, that exile had turned into plain oblivion. But that was not true: Sara never forgot that her sister was living in a cell for having poisoned the man who was going to make her happy. Madame Michaud, for her part, could not feel the guilt they attributed to her, or any repentance for her actions: her universe did not allow for such possibilities, because it was not a human one; things are not guilty, and constructions do not feel repentance. It's a cliché to say that she lost track of time; but the prison guards said she rarely went out into the yard and hardly ever associated with the other convicts, and that she lived, in all other respects, at the margin of any evolution, ignorant of the routines of the world inside and the revolutions outside. Enclosed in the minimal space of her cell, Madame Michaud did not hear that her mother died of natural causes during the winter of 1969, and never found out that, on her deathbed, she'd forgiven her. Would this pardon have made her glad? It's impossible to know for certain. Her cellmate, who very soon exhausted her longings for conversation, tells that Madame Michaud (whose hair turned gray, whose transparent skin dried and peeled like birch bark) spent the days rolling and unrolling a piece of paper over the floor of the cell. On one side of it was printed an old calendar brought from France: 1954—DIXIÈME ANNIVERSAIRE DE LA LIBÉRATION was the caption set above the months and days. On the back of the calendar, Madame Michaud had drawn a pencil sketch of Les Houx in such detail that her cellmate exclaimed, when she saw the plan for the first time, that she knew the place. It was not true, but the perfection of the details had prevailed over her memory. The illusion, momentary for the other convict, was complete for Madame Michaud; and she lived her years of imprisonment within that plan, oblivious to her increasing old age. It's not difficult to imagine her bending over windowsills that were a simple thick line, or thinking she was hiding behind walls that were made not of bricks and concrete, but of the careful shading of a slanted pencil.

I imagine it was prisoner Michaud's good conduct that, paradoxically, caused the distraction of the directors of the Charleroi prison. No one, during the final years of her imprisonment, seemed to remember her; and it's easy to believe that many more years would have been commuted had she submitted an official request before. When it was decided she deserved early release, she was six years from completing her sentence. But ten years earlier, the same pardon would have been conceded: her behavior was the same during that whole life within a life that is a murder conviction. In December 1998, Madame Michaud was summoned to the César Franck room of the prison, where she answered a series of questions meant to confirm her willingness to return to and be a useful member of society. At the end of the session, they asked her if she would prefer to get out before or after the holidays: on the brink of freedom, Madame Michaud did not want to spend one single day more in jail. The prison officials placed among her belongings (the toilette she'd arrived with and a calendar on the back of which was the plan of a house) an envelope with three thousand francs in five-hundred-franc notes. On December 19, Madame Michaud spent the night in a Charleroi motel—nobody had been waiting for her outside the prison gates—and before dawn she was ready to return to Les Houx. (At seventy-nine years of age, Madame Michaud no longer slept much, and always awoke with the first light.) She didn't have to explain to the taxi driver where her family's property was.

The taxi drove slowly up the drive, for it had snowed and a layer of ice made the surface slippery. Madame Michaud wiped the condensation from the car window to see the house, her house, and must have thought she'd open the main door and it would be as if not a day had gone by. She didn't dismiss the driver as soon as she stepped out of the taxi, perhaps because she felt that it wasn't gravel beneath the snow but pebbles. But she kept going, and her hand moved instinctively to the place where the large door knocker had always been: her hand fell on emptiness. It must have seemed implausible to her to have to look for the latch, and to have to try twice before being able to get it to open. She had to imagine the possibility that she'd not been paying attention on her way there, that the taxi driver had brought her to someone else's house. She looked around. On her face was confusion. Madame Michaud felt disoriented.

In the front hall, where there had always been a stone angel stationed under the staircase, there was now no staircase, but rather a solid oak bookcase, and the stone angel was an armchair for reading. Three rooms shared the space that thirty-nine years earlier had been the living room: one for the hunting weapons, one for winter clothes, and another that Madame Michaud did not verify, because it looked dark and perhaps deep (she thought there was a banister descending to a cellar), and she was afraid of getting lost. The main floor was unrecognizable; Madame Michaud was consoled by the fact that she could not go upstairs—she didn't know how to get there—thus she avoided having to feel her way blindly again and the unfamiliarity, the painful unfamiliarity.

Madame Michaud was not alone in the house, but the

other presence would not have given herself away for all the gold in the world. From the rose windows of the attic, Sara saw her leave, and it was as if she could feel the cold that stung her older sister's face. Sara did not miss out on a single detail: before her anxious gaze, Madame Michaud saw that a sort of hut without walls stood on the spot where, as she remembered, the barn for the Lusitanian horses had been, and then, with a hand to her forehead, she discovered that the distant garden with its sleeping plants had once been a dense grove of trees. She was grateful that the taxi was still waiting, because she wasn't sure she'd be able to find the way out among so many new lanes leading to so many new outbuildings, to the many recent constructions that Sara had planned and erected with the patience of an artist over the course of thirty-nine years, in many cases not even yet occupied or serving any purpose, because their only justification was to replace a memory or an affection in the mind of Madame Michaud so that now she, in the backseat of the taxi, would be wondering where she might go, what place remained for her in the world.

At the Café de la République

Your name and address are typed on the envelope, as I didn't want you to recognize my handwriting and throw the letter away without even opening it. This is the sentence at the top of the page on which I tell Viviane about what has happened to me over these last few months—without going into too many details about the illness, because I don't even have any myself—and ask her to come with me to visit my father. Now, for the first time since I posted it, I think she might not come, and I feel I wouldn't blame her. I said to meet at the Gare d'Austerlitz—the railway stations are practically the only places in Paris open on Sundays—and I've sat down to wait for her on a bench that smells like bleach and the coffee a tramp is drinking very slowly beside me and the sweat of weekend joggers. The cold has let up a little bit: it's now possible to see people carrying their sweaters as they walk, days are getting longer and dawn now breaks without fog, and the last layer of gritty ice on the sidewalks has melted away. Whole centuries seem to have passed since November. Would these first months of single life or solitude have been the same for her? When I see her coming, I rush over to meet her so she won't have to come into the entrance hall, because she, perhaps the woman most sensitive to cold in existence, is still wearing her overcoat and scarf despite the newspapers saying that winter ended a week ago, and she's always detested going into warm places because of the extravagant unwrapping and wrapping up again involved. I don't know how I should greet her; she reveals the same awkwardness. We don't kiss. We don't shake hands. Viviane's gaze passes over my shoulders and hair, avoids immediately focusing on the inflammation on my neck. The white and polished midday light bathes her face with a deceptive pallor. I'm not surprised that, six months after our separation, she still strikes me as unusually beautiful. But nobody has ever said we should stop finding a woman attractive once we've left her.

"So, you didn't tear up the letter," I say to her.

"No. But I do want to ask you that we get this over with as quickly as possible."

"You bought some new earrings."

"A couple of weeks ago," says Viviane. "Where are we going?"

"To République. You've been to the apartment, I don't know if you remember."

"Your father's still there?"

"Still there. What's the matter?"

"It can't be healthy. Isn't it full of bad memories, ghosts?"

"Of course," I say. "But they only scare the guests."

"You know what I mean," says Viviane, irritated. "Don't play the fool."

My mother left the apartment on Rue de la Fontaine-au-Roi when I was sixteen years old. Her departure was foretold, and no one held out any hope during her brief resolution to force herself to restore family life: those were the good intentions that anticipate the definitive decision, and that was obvious even to my father. Until we were officially engaged, I hid certain aspects of that process from Viviane. At the time I thought and said that it pained me to touch on the subject; now, that conviction has deserted me. When I finally told her about all that, of the nights when my father would come home drunk and furious with my mother for leaving him and their son, kicking doors and startling me awake in the middle of the night, Viviane reproached me for taking so long to tell her. She complained about my silences, about the walls I seemed to put up around myself. She complained about not feeling needed. Referring to my mother, she said, in a moment of rage, that I had probably been happy about it, because all my life I'd been happy when I was able to do without someone: an occasional girlfriend I decided not to see anymore, a friend who silently drifted away until he stopped talking to me, guests whose stay was reaching its end. She was always disturbed by the ease with which I excluded others or allowed them to exclude themselves.

We wait for the metro on the Bobigny side. The trains still run aboveground at first. The car we get into is empty, except for two North African women who are sitting on the drop-down seats as if they preferred to be uncomfortable, as if they felt unworthy of the spaciousness of the main benches. Viviane turns away from me, and her face, during the dark stretches between stations, is reflected in the glass as if it were a mirror. Behind that face, deep in the black wall, is mine: suspicious eyebrows, Mediterranean fisherman's nose, bandage. My attention goes back to Viviane. When she squeezes her eyelids shut, I notice she's not wearing any makeup. When we said hello, she'd successfully pretended, but now that talent is beginning to evaporate.

"Please don't cry," I say.

"Why not? So your father won't imagine things?"

I don't say anything. I don't want this day to start with an argument.

"Don't you think he's going to realize we're not together anymore?"

Her resentment toward me is visible, and it's obvious she's been nurturing it with dedication. At first, months earlier, I used to stop and wonder what Viviane was feeling, what questions were going through her mind, or what sorrows, what things she'd be regretting. I soon stopped, out of fear of the small private abyss that this solidarity opened in front of me. Lovers are not made for pondering the consequences of their own actions. Viviane asks me:

"How long has it been since you last saw him?"

"A year, more or less. There's no reason he would have found out about us. So this is the favor I'm asking of you."

"I already know that, don't hassle me so much. Leave me alone for a while, please."

She looks at me. The sadness in her eyes is almost intolerable. It hurts her to be with me, see me, and hear my voice for the first time in four months. If she agreed to come, I think, it's because she knows as well as I do how much her presence facilitates relations with my father, and because she understands my desire to avoid explaining anything, describing my life, going into my reasons for leaving her: she understands, in fact, that I'd rather give my father the impression that my family is intact and that the son of a wife who left will not inevitably abandon his own marriage. We've been talking in shouts, as people do so the roar of the metro won't carry away their words, and the women looked at us out of the corners of their eyes, as if through their veils. I feel like insulting them. Then I realize they're looking at my face, not a banal dispute between former lovers. Viviane has also noticed, and with the hand still wearing her wedding ring—or has she put it back on this morning, perhaps she was even lucid enough to think of that—she touches my cheek and jaw and the bandage covering the swollen lymph node. She examines it.

"It might not be anything serious, right? It *might* be something else."

I say yes, the doctors don't know yet.

"I hope you're not lying to me."

"I explained everything in the letter, Viviane," I say, letting my head drop. "Can we not overdramatize this, please?"

"Don't be like that. Look at me."

I obey.

"That's better," says Viviane. "You're ill, I have a right to worry."

This encounter must be much more difficult for her than it is for me. She has no hidden motives; I, however, am thinking all the time about this visit I've decided to pay, and for which Viviane is instrumental. Perhaps she's now grown used to my absence, after who knows what efforts, and then I show up and write to her asking that we see each other again. I want to question her: Have you gotten used to it? Viviane, have you stopped loving me? I don't, perhaps because it would be an awful way of playing dirty. I want to play fair with Viviane. I owe her a lot, and I know it. I thank her for coming, for putting up with this. But at the very moment I speak, the car fills with noise, because the train has gone into a tunnel.

"What did you say?" she asks me.

"Nothing, nothing," I say. "I like it better when the train is aboveground."

Viviane doesn't reply.

"Here we are." I nudge her gently with my fingertips. "We have to get off here."

Of course I am ashamed of my cowardice; I don't know if the harm I'm doing to Viviane is justified. But seeing my father is, today at least, a necessity. When we come up outside, my shoes are heavy as if I were walking on sand.

FIVE WEEKS after leaving Viviane, while reading an uninteresting essay by Georges Perec one night, I felt a hardness under my jaw. Bending my chin down, as one often does when reading in bed, I felt like I had a glass marble stuck to my skin. I spent the whole night bending my neck, lowering my chin, moving my head; discovering all the positions in which the marble made its presence known. Up till then I had never been ill: illnesses were things that happened to other people, someone else's anecdotes or passing difficulties. A week later, after blood tests had been done, when each doctor whom another doctor referred me to evaluated the same symptoms and asked the same questions about pain, about my family medical history and possible fatigue, I began to experience a new sensation. As I crossed Paris by metro for another appointment or to pick up the results of the latest test, I was afraid, because each time a doctor touched my throat, I felt certain—it was an exaggerated but not entirely false certainty—that the marble had doubled in size. I was afraid because all the doctors asked me to undress, although for me it was a simple inflammation in a place that had nothing to do with my armpits, my elbows, the backs of my knees, or the flesh of my abdomen, and, nevertheless, the doctors pressed all over, with their fingers of greenish latex, looking for other inflammations. The first time this happened, a young doctor on Avenue de la Motte-Picquet told the woman who had recommended him to me what she then told me over the phone later that day. I don't know if he confided in her with the express intention that she would repeat it to me, almost word for word, as she in fact did. "Xavier says that you shouldn't worry too much. If it really is cancer, we're going to find out relatively quickly."

That was not the case: we did not know relatively quickly. The diagnoses continued to be imprecise, and I continued to walk around Paris—now almost all the doctors I saw were in the 15th arrondissement, which, at least, meant I didn't have to spend the whole day underground in the metro—with the feeling that something was getting away from me: time, the city I was beginning to hate, the simple truth, daily calm. Unidentifiable lytic detritus, the detection of macrophages, all this was like a keyhole, barely suggesting the illness with a hermeticism resembling poetry. People's curious glances soon began to try my patience. But then I'd get home, look in the mirror, and forgive them, for it was impossible to pretend that the deformity on my face might not attract attention. It had transformed into half a sphere, as prominent as if someone had sewn a pocket onto my left jawbone, and it was tender and the skin covering it was a lighter color, milky like the water in a puddle. I was tormented by the lack of symmetry, the bulge I'd occasionally catch sight of on my shadow, the hindrance if I looked back over my left shoulder; but more than anything else, my lost invisibility, the notoriety my face acquired in any public place. I was no longer nobody, now I was *a person* among the abstract assembly of *people* in the metro. I didn't know, until that moment, the importance I gave to the possibility of being incognito, and now, suddenly, everybody I crossed paths with on the street was like a relative who looked at me from afar until realizing, by the time they were at my side, that no, we'd never seen each other before. I learned to hate. At a pedestrian crossing at the Jardin du Luxembourg, a woman waiting beside me to cross Rue de Vaugirard approached me to ask, point-blank, what that was I had on my face; the youngest daughter of Madame Schumer, my landlady, refused to greet me with a kiss, and her expression revealed disgust and fear at the same time. She was an eight-year-old girl, but I felt contempt for her (and for all the rest of the children I saw outside, clean and healthy, unaware of their bodies) and avoided her from then on.

The same day I had a chest X-ray and an MRI, I received a call I didn't get to in time because I was in the shower trying to wash the blue gel the doctor had smeared on the scanner wand off my neck and chest: a cold lubricant that left me feeling, on the way home, that my cotton clothes were constantly sticking to my skin, not like sweat, but like dry nectar. The absurd possibility that it had been my father calling lodged in my head. It was absurd, because he didn't know I was no longer married, didn't have my new phone number, and knew nothing of my indecipherable illness; it was absurd, above all, because my father never had any reason to want to talk to me. Now, imagining it had been him who called seemed unusual for me, almost fantastical, except for the fact of probable death. In the cinema, walking along the Canal Saint-Martin, over breakfast, the probability I was dying of lymphatic cancer had begun to dog me. Maybe I still had a few doctors to consult; I still hadn't received test results proving it irrefutably, but I had already stopped feeling I had more than enough time.

A couple of days earlier, then, I made up my mind. I'd just undergone the last tests: several punctures that extracted a sepia-colored liquid from the swollen lymph node, a liquid that would be left to ferment for three days on a saucer like the ones we used in school to separate salt from water, and which would, according to Dr. Fauchey, give us fundamental information about the nature of my illness. I didn't actually see the instrument used: I felt a sharp itch but no real pain, because the skin covering the node lost sensitivity and became almost dead tissue. While I was waiting for the results, I went out for a walk through Montparnasse, perhaps trying to catch a little of Parisians' feigned frenzy, but my impatience obliged me to look for a pay phone and call the doctor. His secretary answered; she said that Fauchey was out of town until the weekend. "Call him on Monday," the woman had said, and I felt something like hatred toward her. "Does the doctor have a mobile?" I asked, and heard a no, first of all, and then a long silence on the other end of the line. "Give me that number," I said. "I might have . . . I might be very ill and not know it. It'll be your responsibility, mademoiselle." The threat was infantile, but effective. The strange thing was my difficulty in pronouncing the name of my possible illness. For some time now the word itself, seen by chance in the display window of the Odéon medical bookshop or even in a magazine horoscope, would provoke slight dizziness and an empty feeling in my stomach.

I dialed Fauchey's number three times. A recording kept saying the telephone was switched off or out of range.

Then I phoned my father. I put up with his preliminary sarcasm, the indirect complaints about my absence—he asked if I was coming to take revenge after my banishment to the Isle of Ur—and I put up with the terrible excuses he offered for not seeing me: activities he gave up after my mother left, seeing friends who'd gradually left him alone since he started drinking. I didn't hang up, despite his comments, and maybe that's why my proposal had an air of a considered resolution, not of affection or nostalgia, impressions that would have provoked his flight.

"I was planning to stay home this weekend anyway," he'd told me. "Come on over, bring your wife and a bottle of whiskey."

My father's building is in a neighborhood of cobbled streets, which is nonetheless hostile and dark. There's lots of graffiti, but not the ingenious epigrams you might see in other cities around the world, more like abstract signatures that look a bit like battle crests. The apartment has plaster walls, and the neighbors' moans of pleasure or confrontations are, more than merely audible, shameless or intrusive. I hear, before knocking on his door, the movements of a tired body. My father has aged: he is no longer the man whose solidity was visible in the strength of his back, in the determined and sure expression in his Bedouin eyes. In his youth he was a boxer; I never learned to raise my fists, and as soon as I had enough words to invent my own philosophy, I considered him barbarous and atavistic for wanting me to assume poses seen on a Greek amphora. But I never told him that; I'd never had the courage to confront him in ways that obliged me to hold his gaze. When he opens the door, I think he doesn't look like he's been drinking, and the fear that his behavior will shock Viviane, or make her regret even more having come with me, disappears. My father is wearing a brown corduroy overcoat with patches on the elbows and twill cotton trousers of a vague gray. *"Les enfants,"* he greets us. But he does not invite us in.

"I feel like going out," he says. "There's a café here on the corner as bad as any other."

We go back down the stairs, following him. He's losing his hair: a sparse patch is visible among the gray curls on his head. I point it out to Viviane; she nods and smiles a little. From the other side of a wall we hear the voice of a man saying something in a language I didn't understand.

"Fucking gypsies," says my father. "When will they get used to talking like normal people. Did you walk here?"

He doesn't look at us when he asks this question, and I don't immediately realize he means us.

"No, we took the metro, monsieur," Viviane says.

"Lazybones," says my father. "How can you go down into that filthy tube on a day like this?"

The owner of the Café de la République, I discover, knows my father as well as a lifelong friend. He himself opens the door for us, and the four of us walk to a corner table wedged between the slot machine and the Formica counter, at the back. The coppery mirrors reflect a stained image back at us.

It's obvious this is my father's table: whenever he arrived somewhere for the first time, he worried about where to sit, saying that customers who waiters identify with their own tables get better service, get to make calls—the telephone is an old-school model that still accepts coins—and can use the washroom even if they haven't ordered anything. Only once we're sitting down does my father ask me what's on my neck.

"Nothing, a little swelling," I tell him. "I'm on antibiotics, it'll be fine."

He doesn't ask anything more. His curiosity has been satisfied.

It's been so long since I last saw him that I've almost lost the habit of feeling intimidated: experiencing that sensation again might have annoyed me, but today timidity is far away, separated from me like a frog pinned out, ready for dissection. My father begins by ordering three glasses of cider—he doesn't consult us, doesn't ask what we want—and the serious stuff soon begins. A bottle of Four Roses appears on the glass table, among viscous circles and cigarette ash.

Viviane, aware that her role consists of filling with dialogue the silences that have always flowed between my father and me, begins to talk. Her talent for choosing phrases, for showing interest in other people's concerns without appearing contrived or fake, for expressing sharp opinions on matters totally alien to her, has never ceased to surprise me. She tells my father he should go back to journalism, asks him if he doesn't miss contact with reality.

"The problem is that reality's a penniless whore," he says. "People complain because the papers manipulate information and all that, but the truth is that reality couldn't care less, as long as it gets well paid for being written about."

He lifts his glass of whiskey to his lips, and the slot machine lights blink in the liquid and turn it into a urine sample for medical tests.

"That's why it's better to devote yourself to fiction, like this one."

I haven't devoted myself to fiction. I've published one travel book, after a short journey around Tibet, and the royalties have allowed me to pay the rent punctually and go to the cinema occasionally, and I get by, in the meantime, thanks to the contract I've signed for two more books. My father is a man who always wanted to write, and didn't manage it. He worked as a journalist, first conducting conventional interviews for *Libération* and then, before my mother's departure, writing more personal *crónicas* (literary chronicles, they used to be called) with the devotion of someone who's just discovered his destiny. He must have read cheap translations of Tom Wolfe books dozens of times, and ended up writing two or three pieces his colleagues respected. Then, one Saturday as we were coming back from the racetrack, my father began to speed up a couple of blocks from home. I don't know how he guessed, or if some specific fact allowed him to link a chain of coincidences ending with the incredible deduction that, over the course of that morning, my mother had left. But when we got to our building, he had only to greet the concierge to imagine what the mailbox would have confirmed. He didn't even bother to open her parting letter. He already knew what it said, he told me later: it was the same as his last arguments with my mother.

He stopped working for several months. He ran out of money; the pressure of his obligations weighed heavily on him. Then something resembling a resurrection occurred, because he returned to the *Observateur* with a magnificent story on the most notorious fraud in the history of French sport. A popular singer, known to gamble, was implicated, as was a former functionary of de Gaulle's government. I don't remember how much he got paid for that article, but it was an excessive sum; offers began to arrive from all over, and I remember finding envelopes from *Esquire* and *Harper's* in the mailbox. One day, his editor came to see him at home. I opened the door. A man in jeans, a silk shirt, and a jacket with patches on the elbows came in and said hello to my father. "Letters have arrived at the magazine," he said. "I need to verify the facts in your text or we're going to get sued."

"I don't understand," said my father. "What do you mean?"

"Don't look at me like that, man, I'm not questioning anything. Pierre hasn't been able to verify your facts or find the informants you quote."

"But I did. I found them and I talked to them. I thought you were on my side."

"In the article you mention a hotel. You interviewed your main source there, the guy from the Olympic Committee, or whatever it was. Anyway, the one who knew all about the fraud."

"Yes. That one."

"Which hotel was it?" said the editor. "I need you to take me there. I need someone, a waiter, a bellboy, anyone, to recognize you."

"It was the Ibis. The Ibis at the airport."

"That's what we thought. From the noises you describe in the text. But we called, and they have no record of a guest by the name of your source, and nobody remembers seeing anyone interviewed in the lobby."

"All right, all right. It wasn't in that hotel."

"In the article you say it was."

"That was to protect him. You saw the information the guy gave me. I wasn't going to publish his address. *Merde*."

"Don't get upset. Just give me his phone number."

"I don't have it."

"Tell me where he lives."

"I don't know," said my father. "It was a while ago, I don't keep files on the people I interview."

The editor lowered his voice, as if what he was about to say was disgraceful to him, more than to my father.

"That piece is pure bullshit, and you know it. I'll see you tomorrow at the office."

They did not see each other at the office, because my father sent a resignation letter so he wouldn't have to wait to be asked. By then, he had started drinking; the incident did nothing but confirm his reputation. A little while later, when I told him I was looking for student accommodation in Nanterre, he said: "I thought so. The rats are always the first to abandon a sinking ship." I made excuses: it was true in part that I was sick of the daily trip from Paris to the university—the desolate cars of the RER, the crowds of sad men and women coughing over the previous day's newspapers—but he was determined to believe that I despised his failure and was leaving him to sink alone. He never said so, of course. I had to interpret, to deduce it, as usual, from various comments here and there.

"So, how's the fiction going, then?" asks my father.

I know he's not expecting an answer. I think of saying *I'm not the one who writes made-up things, Papa.* But I don't.

"Fine," I say at half volume. "It's going."

My father stands up and we watch him walk toward the washroom. He leans on the backs of chairs, on the shoulder of a shaven-headed teenager who's playing pinball, and on the doorknob, which is meant to look like an uncut diamond, a plastic prism so opaque that light does not reflect off it.

"He's an expert," I say. "I've never seen anyone so adept at the art of walking while drunk."

"He's already drunk?" asks Viviane.

"Of course he is. Don't tell me you hadn't noticed."

"Well, he's a charming drunk, your papa. The exact opposite of what you always told me."

"What did I tell you?"

"You told me physical strength. You told me moral weakness. But what I see is quite different. Of course, it's only the second time I've ever met him, or the third."

"You're right. It's just that I barely know him."

Viviane smiles. I get impatient.

"Now what?"

"The two of you make me laugh," she says. "Your irony, your sarcasm. Even if you don't admit it, you've inherited all that."

I interrupt her: I'd rather avoid the psychology I used to get so often when we were a couple. I ask her, instead, how she is, how she's been feeling. Viviane sets her glass down on the table.

"I don't want to talk about us. This is not going to happen again, so it's not something you should get used to."

"I didn't . . ."

"I came with you today because I know it's important, or at least I believed what you said in your letter. But that's as far as it goes. Don't come looking for me again."

"Understood."

"Understood?"

"Yes, Viviane. Understood."

"Okay, now, tell me something. Is it true you're on antibiotics?"

"Of course not. I don't even know what I have."

"Ah, okay. Because I was going to say you shouldn't be drinking any whiskey if you're on antibiotics, let alone as much as this."

Viviane has suddenly adopted a lighthearted, playful attitude, as if she wanted to forget about the bandage over my lymph node. The whiskey is an indispensable factor, of course. But Viviane's behavior, by way of the brief alcohol-induced euphoria, is genuine and transparent. I've always liked that about her: there are no strategies or double intentions in Viviane. She is a woman who says what she thinks and never keeps things that need to be said to herself. Perhaps—I can't say I hadn't considered it—leaving her had been one of those mistakes that nothing can rectify. And for a while now that fear has been joining the others, and I've often wondered if I'd lost her by now, if I'd lost her forever. And then I don't know if I'm frightened by the words or the fact of being stuck in the middle of the reality they describe. Mistake. Forever. Lost. Words like these scare me more than anything else.

When my father gets back, Viviane takes his arm to help him fall onto his chair, precise and rough like the ballast of a balloon.

"I wanted to ask you a favor, monsieur," Viviane says, filling all three glasses up to the top. "Tell me about your son, tell me about his childhood. He's so secretive, it's impossible to get him to talk about himself."

"Well, if this is how things are going, I'll get lost," I say. "Nobody's going to force me to sit through this torture. Besides, I have to make a call."

Above my father's upper lip are white specks. His facial hair is dense and coarse, and when he's shaved inattentively, like today, it's inevitable that bits of toilet paper and loose threads from a napkin get stuck to his face. As I stand up and walk away toward the telephone, I hear him say:

"Agreed, my dear. But first, let's order a nice steak. I'm starting to need some food to go with this drink."

THE FINAL DAYS of our marriage passed by in the midst of a perfidious affability, at least on my part. I was attracted to Viviane; I hadn't lost interest in her conversation; she wasn't docile, but she knew how to make me feel that spending time with me satisfied her, which is perhaps the highest tribute a lover can hope for. I, for my part, used absurd euphemisms to name the rift or absence I'd begun to feel, those words that explode if you're not careful, like a box of fireworks or a father-son relationship. On the morning of November 6 last year—I remember the date because a local magazine ran a devastating review of my book that day, not criticizing the book but rather my father, the man who had faked an article years earlier—that morning, as I said, as I watched her from bed, I knew as if someone were whispering it in my ear that we no longer had much time left together. I sat up in bed, all my senses focused on this woman. Viviane never closed the bathroom door (she always teased me about my exaggerated modesty) and now, unexpectedly, she was a Pierre Bonnard figure, a faceless woman drying her legs with a towel the color of tropical fruits, or rather the towel was caressing her, encircling her thighs, preparing the surface of her skin for the application of seaweed moisturizer. Never had I liked a woman this much: Why was I thinking of leaving? It had been her idea to travel to Tibet, as long as we could find a hotel where they spoke French or English. She was the one who banned me, during the time it took to write the book, from getting distracted by banal articles, saying we could easily live on her salary from the importer for a short time. Perhaps that had been the only thing I'd been sure of lately: without Viviane, I would never have finished that book. And in spite of that, there I was, sitting cross-legged on top of the sheets of the un-made bed, receiving the scent of her deodorant and the steam from the shower, watching her and desiring her and thinking of leaving her. My forehead was damp and so were my palms, and it took me a few seconds to understand: neither the steam nor the radiators were to blame. I was sweating.

Noticing I was watching her, Viviane fastened the towel around her waist like a man—she knew that few things could excite me as much as seeing her like that—and came back into the bedroom to get dressed. Our bedroom was narrow. A map of the world covered the widest wall; on the IKEA bedside table Viviane had a vase sometimes containing an iris and sometimes a sprig of chamomile. She chose a blue sports bra: she was going to have to do a lot of walking over the course of the day, up and down lots of stairs in the metro. The previous day she'd brought me a gift of an unvarnished pinewood shelf to put up on the wall, beside the closet, for my first editions; this morning, turning to tell me something, she banged her head on the shelf to which her body had not yet become accus-tomed. We laughed, but the impact was a hard one, and the screws crunched and a goose egg came up on Viviane's fore-head. I made her sit down on the bed, went to get some cotton balls and iodine, and improvised some modest first aid. I said good-bye to her at the door with a kiss to her forehead, and felt on my lips the heat and roughness of the grazed skin damaged by the blow.

Right afterward, repeating the whole time (as if someone might be listening) that I needed exercise, I put on a gray sweatshirt, stuffed a couple of white T-shirts in a knapsack we'd bought in a temple in Jokhang, and jogged down the five flights of stairs. My body decided on its own to take Rue Monge toward Gobelins, and I kept jogging without feeling the muscles in my legs, leaving behind the tiny apartment Viviane and I had lived in since our marriage. I was alone, even in the midst of the people who crowded the sidewalks, and I recognized the privilege of that solitude. I tried to imagine the feeling of absolute certainty, separate from the desire I felt for Viviane, and that destroyed our relationship because it was accompanied by the fear of abandonment; I thought of the feelings I'd discovered when I left my parents' house—or my father's, who was living alone by then—yes, that was certainty, that was absolute confidence, for dependence on someone else would no longer intimidate me and neither would the fear of looking at my reflection in the mirror one day and seeing what I saw in my father's eyes: imbalance in the black iris, the shining cornea of men who are lost.

I didn't stop until I no longer recognized the neighborhood around me, and even then I didn't stop completely. I must have walked for more than half an hour, first along Port-Royal and later through Montparnasse. Then I leaned on the back wall of the Hôpital Necker—where later I would go for an MRI—and tried to weigh up my life that afternoon or plan an itinerary, to keep my head from falling into an uncontrollable disorder or to name what had just happened, with the terrible awareness we get once we've hurt the person we love. On the corner of Rue du Cherche-Midi, a woman with purple hair and a mink coat was sweeping up her dog's excrement.

"WAIT A MINUTE," says Viviane, laughing her head off. "I'm dizzy, I need to stop for a second."

We're at the entrance to Jussieu, the closest station to the apartment I don't live in anymore. Viviane has few inherited traits, but one of them is some kind of middle-ear disorder that makes her vulnerable to the most unexpected bouts of dizziness. When she has too much to drink, the symptoms get mixed up, and sometimes the situation gets so serious that she has to sit down—on the floor of the shower, in the middle of the street—and just pray for the world to stop spinning.

"You want to know what I think?" I ask her. "I think the princess has a very refined palate. The princess can only drink Lagavulin's, that's the thing."

"You talk like you know what that is," Viviane says.

"Well, neither do you."

"You've never even seen a bottle that good," she says.

"Neither have you," I say.

"But friends of mine have," she says. She waits a moment and adds: "There is something you don't know."

"What's that?"

"I masturbated yesterday. For the first time since you left."

Viviane laughs. I laugh, too, an accomplice to her game.

We've left my father lying on his bed. The effort required to get him up the spiral stairs has not been negligible. Viviane got lost under his left arm, I was carrying his head on my shoulder like a marble bust. The smell of his metallic breath has stayed on my clothes, that mixture of whiskey, toothpaste, and betel nut. Before we left the Café de la République, my father began to hum "Février de cette année-là," the song he chose to learn by heart a long time ago, before an interview with Maxime Le Forestier that never took place in the end. By the time we covered him with his yellowing bedspread—Viviane had instinctively shaken it out, and the lightbulb at the entrance transformed the dust into floating flour—he'd started repeating the same bit of the tune over and over again, and Viviane, taking pity on him, filled out his monotonous delivery with any old line here and there, *Tu peux venir chez moi,* or perhaps *Les yeux pleins de brouillard.* Still beside the bed, she asked me in a whisper if my mother had slept on this same mattress. I confessed that I hadn't noticed and would never notice that sort of detail, but it always seemed normal to me that she did. Then my father grabbed my hand, squeezed it between both of his, and said:

"Come back on another day."

And then, in a harsher tone:

"Not for your sake, though. It's your wife, who does actually know how to carry on a conversation like friends from the old days."

Now we're walking down the streets we've walked together thousands of times, arriving from somewhere to the bed that used to be ours and no longer is. I look at the windows of the buildings on our street, and I think how the lives of others fascinate people and that perhaps somebody, at this very moment, is spying on us from behind a half-open blind, and is pleased to see us together again, to see Viviane with a spring in her step like before. And that person will not think of my confusion or my sadness, because I'm the one who chose to leave.

"I've passed by here so many times," I say. "I've thought of coming to see you, to find out how you were."

"And your knees shook, I imagine." Viviane bursts out laughing. "It's true, your cowardice is beyond redemption."

When we get to the apartment, I notice that Viviane has not let herself go, that her life has not given way to incoherence. In the sink is just the small breadboard with traces of honey and hazelnut spread and the fuchsia-colored plastic glass from this morning's breakfast; there are no dirty dishes piling up on the drying rack, no jackets hanging carelessly over chair backs. *Les yeux pleins de brouillard,* sings Viviane. I ask her to change the tune, and she, laughing, says she doesn't remember any others and she likes that one because the mention of fog in the eyes has made her think of a recently awakened Le Forestier, his hair still a mess, rubbing sleep out of his eyes the way I used to before starting to write. I've almost forgotten the unmistakable signs of her contentment, the way she forgot about everyone else when she was happy. She couldn't care less that a guffaw might make her seem rough or masculine; she couldn't care less about her posture.

"I'll be right back to say good-bye," she says on her way into the bathroom. "You don't mind, do you? I won't be two minutes, it's just that I'm about to burst."

I hear her close the door. That's not a familiar sound; the sound of water running out of the cistern, however, is familiar, as Viviane always flushes it to cover her own sounds when there's a stranger in the house. Tonight, I am the stranger. I look around: on top of two boxes of books I haven't had time to collect sits a new lamp, with a silver base and translucent glass; my screwdriver set is open and spread out beside a small revolving CD rack that Viviane had just picked up at a flea market and hadn't put together yet. Everywhere I see signs of a changing life. Every object tells me that the minuscule order I belonged to no longer exists.

Then Viviane reappears.

"Okay, that's better."

"Are you still dizzy?"

"I had a lot to drink, but don't worry, I'll be fine."

"You'll be fine tomorrow."

"Yes," says Viviane. "Tomorrow I'll be better, but I did drink a lot. I still feel a little drunk."

We could make love, and we both know it. There is a sort of impunity in the air, as if the whiskey we drank and the visit with my father—in which no one embarrassed the other, nor have there been insults or old reproaches—might allow us this small luxury. I sense our fear, and remember having once thought that our love was a shared fear of being alone. Now, the exaltation we feel needs, like any crime, a barely perceptible push. Somehow, I know that Viviane hasn't slept with anyone since we split up. We could make love and tomorrow we could pretend it had been an accident. I could even stay the night here; it would be, for a few hours, as if nothing had changed in our lives.

"I told you not to get in touch again," says Viviane. "But I want you to call me when you get the test results."

"All right."

"Only if you want to, of course."

"Yes," I say. "I'll call you."

Then it happens. I've seen it coming from a long way off, like a crash of locomotives. Viviane's face has crumbled meticulously; the precision of her successive sorrows has been a painful spectacle. She starts to cry, and when I hug her and ask her what's wrong, she keeps crying, as if the distress were a tangle of wool caught in her throat.

"Calm down," I say. "What's the matter, calm down."

"I came with you today."

"Yes." I stroke her hair. "Thank you, Viviane."

She pulls away from me.

"Why didn't you tell me?"

"Tell you what?"

"You know full well, don't play the fool. I would rather not have spied on you, but now I'm glad."

While she was talking about my childhood in the Café de la République, I called Dr. Fauchey from the pay phone. I heard the irritation in his voice, asking how I got his cell phone number, cursing his patients in general for the habit of interrupting his days off. After all that, he said *tubercular infection* and he said *triple treatment, nine months.* And I repeated each of these words as if they were a mantra against the evil eye. The infection was severe, the treatment was going to be expensive and serious; but it wasn't what we'd feared. Fauchey asked: Had I undergone any abrupt changes in environment or diet? Had I been emotionally off balance, depressed? I answered no, none of that. The side of the phone was decorated with propaganda for the '98 World Cup and the national lottery. My fingers scratched at the stickers, and shreds of blue, white, and red plastic like fish guts got lodged under my nails.

"I don't really know why I didn't tell you straightaway. Everything was fine without talking about that, we were happy." I pause and say: "I can't believe you followed me like that, secretly."

"If we were still living together, I wouldn't have done it. That's the most ironic thing. All those stupid ideas about respecting the other person, not listening to each other's conversations, not opening each other's mail, it's pure bullshit, you know?"

"The day was going well, Viviane. I forgot that I'm not with you and I got some good news. And I was able to be with my father."

Then Viviane's eyes opened wide. She'd found the magic formula, the alchemist's secret.

"Don't tell me . . ."

"What?"

"Were you saying good-bye?"

"Not at all." I tried to smile. "Medical science has come a long way."

"Don't give me that. Were you? Did you think—"

"Let's make love."

"And what about me? Settle outstanding scores? Oh, please, how tacky. And you thought I wasn't going to notice, you'd have to be pretty naive."

"Let's make love, Viviane."

"Why can't we be together?"

The sound of footsteps reaches us from the stairs.

"Wouldn't it be easier if we were together?"

"Don't start," I say. "It's not that simple."

"Wouldn't you like me to come with you to your appointments, open the envelopes and read you the results? Wouldn't you like me to be by your side when they tell you on the phone that you're not going to die?"

Odile, the next-door neighbor, arrives every Sunday at the same time. I know (because she told me herself once in the elevator) that she's coming back from Compiègne, where she visits her boyfriend who's been trying to earn a transfer to Paris for years. We both hear her huffing, getting out her keys, turning locks. Viviane turns on the light over the sink, lets the water run, and rinses her eyelids with delicate little pools that collect in her palms. She stays standing there, her back to me. She starts to speak. She doesn't look at me but she starts speaking to me.

"What shoes do you have on?"

It takes me a second or two to catch on. I feel awkward as I look down at my feet, realizing I don't remember having chosen what to wear this morning. Viviane repeats the question:

"Tell me. What shoes did you put on this morning?"

"The red ones. Why do you ask?"

"You bought those shoes on a Sunday. Your book had just come out, I think it was that same week, and the publisher hadn't even paid you the advance. But that morning, while we had breakfast, we made plans to go bowling on Rue Mouffetard. And then you said: I like bowling, but I like bowling shoes even more. I said you should buy some. I told you I'd seen secondhand shoes in Porte de la Chapelle market, and that some of them were colored, like bowling shoes. What did you say to me?"

"I don't remember."

"You said that was all very well, but you didn't have money to spend on colored shoes. What did I say? Do you remember?"

"You said . . ."

"I said you should give yourself an advance on your advance. That you'd earned it for working so hard on your book. That I loved you, and I was proud of you."

She says all this without looking at me, with her voice echoing off the tiled wall. Then she turns around.

"I saw an interview with you. Before Christmas, I think. Do you know the one?"

I know exactly which one. It's the kind of interview I detest: the journalist peppers me with a list of prepared questions, and I have to answer each with one sentence, as if it were a test of mental agility. But Viviane doesn't wait for me to reply.

"They asked you what your happiest memory was. You talked about the day we went up to Lake Yamdrok, said the sky was the same color as the water and that made you feel free. Right?"

She was right.

"Well, that's a lie. Your happiest memory is from when you were a child. You were about ten, maybe. It was New Year's Eve, and one of the neighborhood drunks went out to fire shots in the air just for the hell of it. Your father went out, took the pistol, and knocked him to the ground with one punch. You didn't see him do it, but your friends told you the next day. They seemed to respect you more. But that wasn't the important thing, it was the fact of feeling invulnerable if you were at home and your father was with you. That night you asked him to let you sleep with him. It was the only time he said yes."

Viviane takes a deep breath. She suddenly looks tired. It's not immediate, but an accumulated weariness, as if she hadn't slept for a week. I take a step toward her. I touch her hair.

"I know you inside out," she says. "It's as if I'd lived inside you. I know why you do everything you do. But when you left I felt lost, I didn't know what was happening, I had no one to explain it to me."

My fingers get tangled up in her hair. I close my eyes, recognizing the rootedness of my hands in this movement.

"At first I hated you, you know? I thought you were cruel. I kept telling myself you didn't deserve someone like me. Then I thought I was worthless. If I was unable to keep someone like you, I must be worthless. I was in love with you, that's what it was. I still love you, of course, but before I loved you more than my own life. I don't care if what I say sounds corny to you, I'm not a writer. That's what I felt, that was—"

I kiss her. I don't know if I kiss her so I won't have to hear any more of her words, because each one of them hurts me and harms me. But I kiss her. It's a quick kiss, barely a meeting of lips: Viviane puts her hand on my chest, gently, as if picking up a little bird off the floor, and pushes me away.

"I'd like to stay tonight," I say quietly.

"You are not made to be with me. In fact, you're not made to be with anybody."

I think of my father's eyes. The black iris, the shining cornea. I no longer hear Odile, the neighbor. She must be asleep, happy because she's just spent the weekend with her boyfriend, impatient because she won't see him for another five days.

"You better go," says Viviane. "Tomorrow you'll have to go to a pharmacy, I imagine, begin your treatment. We made a good couple. But you better go."

It occurs to me that this might be the last time I see her. I feel sick for an instant, and my hand, as if by instinct, covers my lymph node. It's a new movement: a sick man is an animal who learns new tricks. Sometimes, this gesture is a response to shame; other times, however, it's a simple nervous tic. Like straightening my glasses on the bridge of my nose. Like touching Viviane's hair. But now it's time for me to go, although part of me doesn't want to.

"Can I call you?" I say.

"Of course not. What for? Your moment of uncertainty is over, isn't it? You're not scared anymore."

I leave. The stairs are dark; before closing the apartment door, I hear her say:

"Now you can go back to being independent."

I PRESS THE SWITCH so a low-watt bulb lights the hallway for twenty seconds. I decide to take the stairs, as I did the last time I was in this building, and press the switches at each floor, and each bulb gives me a brief light, the twenty seconds necessary to get to the next floor and repeat the maneuver. That's how I descend, from one floor to the next, from darkness to darkness, until I feel, as I make it to the sidewalk, the gray and cold of the night like fog in my eyes. I think Paris is small, and that, with a bit of luck, I'll run into Viviane once in a while, at the market or the cinema. They'll be those coincidences that tend to happen in a city like this, falsely grand and rather provincial, a city where people don't often leave their own neighborhoods. I'll see her face, we'll exchange a couple of affectionate phrases. And that's how, bit by bit, I'll go on surviving.

The Solitude
of the Magician

I

What happened inside his pocket struck Léopold as one of the
most extraordinary things he'd ever seen—the interaction of a
wedding band, a key ring, and a hand's magical gesture—and
he could not think it was a mistake, as everyone insisted at
the time, to have publicly questioned a magician's skills, even
just an amateur magician, a mere weekend apprentice. The
magician's face (Léopold remembered the moment when he'd
heard his name, Chopin, and hadn't been able to ask whether
it was a vulgar nickname or a coincidence) emerged from a
thick turtleneck, and the smooth skin under his chin wrinkled when the man nodded or worried, and also wrinkled
when Léopold approached the tallest lamp with the evidence
of magic in his hand and his right heel searched out the switch
on the parquet floor; the light came on and Léopold's eyes

stared at that miracle, a wedding band linked onto a key ring. Selma, his wife, saw him walk toward her, take her left hand, and slip the band, a single diamond set in the gleaming surface, back onto her finger, as if marrying her again, and she couldn't help wondering, given that her marriage still seemed new to her the way shoes you don't wear very often still seem new for quite a while, if this would continue to happen in the future: if small acts or banal circumstances would seem to belong belatedly to the same, now long-ago liturgy.

They had been married in a Catholic ceremony in which her cream-colored, rather than white, bridal gown had caught on the armrests of the seats, because she, willful girl that she was, had insisted the service be held outdoors beside the little stone chapel on the hill that faced Hamoir, in spite of the strong kite-flying wind at that time of year, and all just because it terrified her in the middle of July to be stuck inside the humid and sinister darkness of the Cathedral of Saint Paul, in Liège, with stained-glass windows, grimy with urban grime, that allowed no light through, and a door that on weekends appeared clogged with chocolate and cream *gaufre* stalls and diners' cars and the diners themselves, families of clumsy children with clumsy hands who Selma could already envisage sullying her dress's shimmering train with sweet sticky caramel, apple, or wild blackberry sauces. So Father Malaurie, of Xhoris, used a safety pin to tame his soutane, and blessed the couple without keeping the rice-paper pages of his

Bible from fluttering like a caged bird, without ever finding out that the bride was pregnant, and without knowing, of course, to what extent the pregnancy was one of the most pertinent reasons for her being there that day, holding her veil with her hand so Léopold could kiss her and turning to face the wind so her hair wouldn't tickle the groom's face and make him sneeze at such a solemn moment or get in her eyes. Léopold's kiss tasted of champagne cocktail; the shoulder of his formal suit gave off a whiff of mothballs that Selma reluctantly inhaled. That night she cried a little: she would have liked her father to still be alive to give her away in matrimony. Charles, her father, dead of throat cancer before she learned to speak; her daughter—Selma was magically sure it would be a girl—was fortunate because she'd have a living father, because she wouldn't grow up as lonely as Selma had.

The dream of having a daughter had changed Selma's way of moving, her way of touching Léopold (with whom she'd gone to bed barely a dozen times before a bout of morning sickness had hit her in the middle of Place Saint-Lambert), and later, when they were living together in the house on Rue de Lognoul, near Ferrières, she used to get up in the middle of the night, close the bathroom door so the white light wouldn't wake up her husband, undress in front of the mirror, and lose herself in the contemplation of her body and the changes to her body, because attending to the details of her belly in profile, through the third, fourth, fifth, sixth months, was like watching the phases of a fleshy moon, a fantastic moon with protruding navel against the sky of aquamarine tiles. Her breasts grew until it was possible, by crouching a little in certain positions, to feel her skin resting on her skin, and that sensation, extravagant and at once monstrous, excited her; and her small aureoles darkened and the skin of her nipples hardened and turned porous, two sawdust beauty spots on the pale, round fullness. It was during that time that Léopold offered to host the first hunt of the season, in part for the small honor involved in his group of hunters—men associated with the industrial cleaning company that had maintained his family since 1959—in part for the delicate pride of socially introducing his wife and unborn daughter, one inside the other, a Russian doll. The features of Selma's face were still those that had obsessed Léopold, but the puffy cheeks, the circles under the eyes revealing a certain exhaustion, and her forced smile confounded him, and at the moment of gathering the hunters in a circle for the *maître de chasse* to deliver instructions and lay down the rules, the moment Léopold had planned to bring Selma into the center of the circle and say some calculatedly amusing phrase such as *No shooting any juvenile boars or aiming inside the encirclement, and this, gentlemen, is my wife,* at that moment, dressed in green and gray and with his rifle slung over his shoulder, Léopold only managed to point to her with his gloved hand (it was cold), and in the hush that fell over the cobblestone yard all that could be heard was the hunters' bewildered breaths, the dogs' claws clicking against the cobbles, and the echoes of a piano sonata that someone had left on in the living room filtering through the glass. Then the hunters left, the doors of their four-by-fours banged shut and the dogs barked, and Selma was left alone in the yard. She whistled a few bars of the *Pathétique*: she remembered it because she'd practiced it as a young girl and failed at it. She never managed to understand what her teacher meant when she spoke of the exposition as something that should swirl, or of the transition between the *grave* and the *allegro* as the conversion of a caterpillar into a butterfly. She never liked butterflies; they didn't disgust her, but frightened her absurdly: everyone around her knew this, except Léopold.

When she went into the living room to warm up a little, thinking the cold must not be good for the little girl in her belly, she was surprised to find a stranger sitting in the yellow easy chair, not wearing rubber boots, or hunting gear, or a beater's orange fluorescent jacket, but a wool sweater the collar of which seemed to be folded four times and gave the man the look of a storybook sailor, but a strange sailor, a sailor without a sailor's beard, fond of Alfred Brendel's piano playing and owner of an expression of cynicism or indifferent aversion that had to have been cultivated on dry land. He looked up when he saw her, the woman of the house, come in, and in a display of rudeness that seemed improbable limited his greeting to a nod of the head, not as a sign of welcome, but as if congratulating himself for doing so well what he was doing with his busy hands. And what was that, what were his hands busy with? Selma took a little while to realize that the trail of white linen the man was manipulating was in fact a deck of cards, moving with such speed and such skill, passed from one hand to the other with such dexterity, that from afar and in the gloom of the living room (it was early and no fire had been lit yet) what Selma's eyes managed to see was just a colorless rainbow, and then, when she asked the man to do it more slowly, a succession of pink or gray squares, a blend of white background, and the alternating tones of the figures. It was eight-thirty in the morning; when Léopold came back, just after twelve, he found that his wife had arranged one of the kitchen chairs in front of the corner table from the trophy room and moved Léopold's cast-iron ashtray, Léopold's bi-focals, and the Genevoix book that Léopold was reading so that this Chopin, whom he'd invited simply out of courtesy— since word of the Saturday get-together had gotten out around the office—could not just refuse to go hunting and in passing suggest contempt for the tradition, but also devote himself during the absence of the rest to impressing the hostess with the cheap tricks of an alcoholic gambler or a fairground clown.

Selma, excited and wide-eyed, asked Chopin to repeat two or three of the tricks that had filled the morning's boredom (for him; for her, he'd made time and the heaviness of her belly and the cold and the gray sky of the Ardennes all disappear); he put the deck faceup on the table and asked the youngest beater to think of a card and he turned the deck over and moved the cards from one hand to the other, shuffled twice, put the deck back down on the table, cut the cards, and asked the beater to say what card he'd thought of at the same time as he turned over the top card of the deck. Seven of clubs, said the young man as he picked up the seven of clubs. There was a murmur of voices. Léopold walked across the parquet floor clicking the heels of his waterproof boots and asked if the magician could do something truly bold. Chopin rolled his eyes, perhaps because the same thing had happened to him before and the situation made him uncomfortable; he cut the cards again and asked Léopold to turn over the top card: it was the king of spades, a figure posing in profile with his eye wide open, looking at Léopold with a mocking grimace on his face. Chopin asked the beater to look at his card again: the seven of clubs had turned into the queen of spades and a few people timidly applauded. Then Léopold dared him (maybe he would later wish he hadn't); his voice tried to intimidate, required a real trick, demanded they be impressed.

The magician did not refuse. He asked Selma to take off her wedding ring, and she obeyed; he asked Léopold to show everyone his key chain, a copper stag's head from whose right antler dangled a double metal hoop and the key to his jeep (which flashed when someone lit a match); he walked over to Léopold and, one at a time, dropped both objects into his green corduroy pocket, and then went to stand like a caryatid on the opposite side of the room. From his corner, in front of a bucolic landscape painted in oils by Selma's late father, beneath the head of the first boar Léopold had ever shot—it was in Modave, in 1973, six days before the first snowfall—Chopin pressed his palms together at waist height, said a couple of magic words that sounded atavistic and sardonic at the same time, and his right hand turned over in the air like a dead salamander on the pavement. Léopold felt for the key ring in his pocket: he moved his hand anxiously, almost in fear, among the coins and bullets that fell to the floor when he yanked the copper stag out and showed everyone the tiny frightening miracle: linked on the aluminum hoop, like one more key, was Selma's ring. The guests began to leave. The table was not even set for lunch.

II

Only later, when the accident that was seeded that morning had already taken up its time and its space, when Selma and Chopin had passed through desire and love and shipwreck, would Selma recognize the nature of solitude in the magician's hands. Chopin's hands, small but capable of palming a card— an ace, a queen: yes, especially a hidden queen—lost Selma. The tip of each thumb was covered by a thin, almost invisible callus; on his right hand, another callus bent the first phalange of his middle finger, made it lean slightly out, an elegant hump. Selma would fall in love with his rough fingers, his concealing palms, his wrists so thin that the glass face of watches slipped around to the underside and forced Chopin to look at the time as ladies once did. That very night she asked a couple of questions about Chopin: where was he from—he was from Liège—what was his position in the business—a mere assistant to the underwriter, his office didn't even have a window. This pair of details served to sate her curiosity, but most of all they were useful because she felt that Chopin's name was a raspberry seed stuck in her teeth, something pleasant and annoying at the same time, and talking about him at night, casually from the bathroom, while rubbing stretch-mark-prevention cream into her thighs and buttocks and the moon of rosy skin, was to spit out the seed and sleep in peace. Meanwhile, Léopold reproached her for getting into bed before the cream had dried. It was incredible that she could sleep in sticky, smeared sheets that smelled of laboratory algae.

On Monday, Selma woke up sure that something was burning. While her husband went down to the kitchen to make sure everything was in order, Selma exchanged the intense smell for a ball of nausea the size of a horse's eye, stuck in some part of her trachea that would give no respite. She spent the morning throwing up, the horse's eye refused the most innocent glass of warm milk with honey as she'd always liked it, until her vomit came out yellow and translucent and the heaving finally stopped. For two days it was impossible to stand up without the carpet at the end of the bed beginning to wrinkle and the waves threatening to throw her to the ground if she dared to take a step across it. When the dizziness passed, Selma decided what she needed was air and trees, so on Thursday morning, wrapped in a cotton housecoat over her flannel nightdress and all that covered by a red windbreaker that she hadn't been able to do up over her belly for quite a while, she was giving Heredero the horse his first meal of the day (she was unable to bend over even a little, and had to pour the concentrate from on high as if it were water for the plants), when she heard her husband coming back. He must have forgotten something; he would have realized as he reached the turning onto the highway. Angry with himself, he would have turned around at the traffic lights, on the blind curve that descended toward the valley, swearing and speeding up more than was prudent at such a dangerous point in the Ardennes route. His routine was so rigid that it struck Selma as laughable, so ridiculous to watch him change gears as he pulled onto the highway, first, second, between second and third he would locate the foil package beside the hand brake, between third and fourth, unfold the wrapping and find the Gouda sandwich still steaming; this was his breakfast every day, weekends included, and before getting to Liège he would already have finished it, folded the tinfoil evenly, placed it on the dashboard, covering the speedometer, and he would use it again the next day, and the next, and sometimes for five days in a row. The first time Selma witnessed the routine, Léopold explained it came from his father, a man who'd lived through the war and poverty and after whose death they found fifty cans of preserves, mushrooms, peaches in syrup, plain and pickled herring, forgotten in the back of the cupboard, camouflaged by boxes of contracts and policies and testamentary minutes, which his father had accumulated in case of another war, another German attack. Selma remembered all this as she heard him walking (a careless way of stepping in leather-soled shoes on gravel), breathing as if he were smoking (but the cold air didn't transmit smells very well, or was it that she was monopolized by Heredero's breath), saying hello with a different voice. The fright was momentary but intense: Selma crossed her arms over her inflamed body, protecting her pregnancy. Standing before her, wearing a business suit but no tie—two shirt buttons undone, a hairless chest, the shiny diagonal of a small gold chain—was Chopin. On his face, which was not that of a sailor, was the expression of someone kneeling down before a child to disinfect a graze.

Almost instantly her hands flew to her cheeks and touched her nose, numbed by the cold, and her nose was still in its place, and the same bits of skin on her chapped lips. (Perhaps to confirm that her body still existed, that machine able to feel desire.) Selma went into the stable and turned over the hay at the back, reached inside her jacket, and took out a small white paper rectangle, which she opened with her teeth and emptied onto her glove, held her glove up to Heredero's lips, and wished the horse's tongue would erase her from the world as it erased the sugar from her glove. Nothing happened: nothing wanted to save her. Then Selma must have accepted it, because she began to cross the gravel path (her heavy ankles, thighs full of water, hips asleep under the weight of the baby) and went inside her house through the kitchen and double-locked the door, climbed the carpeted stairs, and only as she reached the last step did she notice the magician's hand was in her hand, not accompanying her, but holding up the unpredictable and oscillating mass of her figure. And at the end of a long gallery of doors, dark because all the rooms were closed so the warm air wouldn't escape, at the end of this strange domestic tunnel in which Selma remembered the trick of the deck expelled from the hand and the chosen card landing in a brandy glass, at the end of the corridor, their passive, concealing accomplice, was the master bedroom that Selma walked into and the matrimonial bed, unmade and still smelling of matrimonial sleep, on which Selma lay down, on her side in the fetal position, perhaps imitating the one she carried inside her. She was already naked when she did so; the naked man came to her from behind, and she discovered almost in a panic that she didn't know what to do with her own arms, perhaps because in this position she'd always put them where her belly now was. Selma felt the heat of another waist against her back, the pubic hair that tickled her buttocks, and felt him penetrate her at the same time she saw the magic hand come over the moon of skin and caress her full breasts, and his index finger, able to shuffle at a vertiginous speed and to feel a card of a fractionally different size in the deck of a cheating magician, played with her protruding belly button. Then the hand clung to the headboard, the magician's open mouth fell onto Selma's shoulder, and she, if she concentrated a little, could feel a thin stream of saliva trickling down her back that might even reach the pillowcase, which she'd have to wash and hang over the bathroom radiators to dry before Léopold came home from work for lunch and afterward felt he'd earned a nap.

III

Very little was known about that man and his reasons for taking a shine to Selma. Years earlier, when he decided to get a degree in Romance languages at the University of Liège, sure that the study of Latin declensions (those miniature spells) would save him from tedium, the professors who interviewed him wanted Chopin to tell them about his childhood, and he summed it up saying he was born in the Esneux hospital and at the age of twelve he'd first managed to throw a card more than thirty meters in an open space, the Quai de Jemmapes, for example, as long as a seagull didn't take it thinking it was food. Between his birth and the flying card it was as if he hadn't existed, he avoided the subject, his face emptied of all presence, and he became mute if someone insisted. He could not bear questions about his parents or when he'd stopped living with them or the way they'd injured him or the qualities, more or less physical, of those injuries, and on the stairways of the main university building, on those worn steps like those of the neon-lit medieval constructions of the amphitheater, he crossed paths with people who mentioned his name and pointed him out and were still talking about him several steps farther down, not the way people talk about a celebrity or a sports star, but expressing surprise, vague admiration, and much pity. Some said that he'd inherited a small fortune, that he lived alone at number 53 Rue de la Loi, and that as a child he'd been an altar boy; others attributed daily visits to Maastricht, the nearest Dutch city on the other side of the border, to buy marijuana where marijuana was legal and cheap, and where he had once put up with threats from a couple of frustrated buyers who refused to understand why Chopin didn't want to sell, especially not to them, a small bag, and who ended up punching him in the stomach. (Before that, the only time anyone hit him outside his home was the afternoon when he guessed, over and over again for more than half an hour, which shell the marble was under on the cardboard table.) When these rumors reached his ears, Chopin slipped into the university projection room and, without turning on any lights, lay down on the floor, between two rows of folding chairs, and lowered the seat board over his head, so the world at that moment became black, blacker than natural black, but also so that over him, near his face, was a surface his breath would bounce off and he could smell it, feel it, breathe it back in again. That made him feel less cold—the smooth brick floor always seemed to be damp—and less afraid, or at least he summoned up the hope, never fulfilled, that later he would go out into a luminous and lived-in world and the simple contrast would determine, by a sort of sorcery, that the other students would forget his existence, or in the worst case would confuse it with one of their own.

Reality (but what reality, if what seemed real to the rest of them was variable and horribly uncertain to him) had undoubtedly played a dirty trick on him. He had never pinpointed exactly how old he'd been when he found, stuck in a train ashtray between Liège and Brussels, a plastic box that his father told him not to touch, saying it was filthy with cigarette butts and slime and maybe bits of rotten food, and which Chopin imagined full of glass marbles or little nails, things that had always helped him pass the time agreeably. The two of them were traveling alone and his father was distracted; with luck he'd forget about the dirty box in the ashtray as soon as the conductor came by to check their tickets—which his father tucked into his shirt cuff so he wouldn't have to go through all his pockets looking for them, mumbling excuses and poking around with nervous hands while the blood invaded the skin between his eyes and beard. But before getting off at Guillemins station, his father picked up the edge of the box with the tips of his immaculate fingers and handed it to the conductor, who looked at it, opened it, and put the transparent lid under the black box and laughed crudely, because inside the box there were no nails or glass marbles but photographs of women (they weren't just photographs, they were something more; but Chopin could not recognize that yet). His father took him by the forearm and they walked together along the platform and down the stairs and through the frenetic tunnel out to the street, the large hand closed around the wool sleeve of his coat, his fingertips scraping the buttons of the cuff as if they were guitar strings. Something happened at that moment, the intuition of a loss: Chopin wriggled out of his father's grip and ran back down the corridor. As he ran up the stairs, his eyes fixed on the sharp edge of each step, he bumped into the man he was looking for, who earned his eternal gratitude and unconditional loyalty by winking at him and sliding into the collar of his sweater the cold rectangle that promised all the excitement in the world and wouldn't just enable him to put up with his father's shouts and the pressure on his sleeve, renewed and more painful than ever, but also provoked true convulsions of emotion when he could at last lock himself in his room, kneel on his bed, untuck his shirt from his trousers to let the new object fall blandly onto one of the red diamonds of his quilt, and it turned out that those diamonds, exquisitely symmetrical and intensely red, were exactly the same as those behind some of the photos, or was it perhaps that the photos were behind the diamonds, not all of them, fortunately. Twenty days later, Chopin had learned how to shuffle; four months would go by before he exchanged his deck for one not adorned with indecent images.

What he did not tell the interviewers, what he never told any other human being, he recounted in detail to the woman he was to save, the woman who was described or prefigured in every movement of his life: his decision not to go to Louvain but to stay in Liège, the idea of putting his name on the municipal youth employment register, accepting the first offer he received after doing so, from an industrial cleaning company. Could anyone think his meeting with the woman feeding horses was not written? Was it possible, if not for the intervention of the good offices of a higher destiny, that a socially inept man like him, with mediocre aspirations and hardly any talent for life, might be allowed to enter the life of such a creature, not to mention be loved by her, touched by her? If anyone had ever told him that one day he would know this kind of lightness in his own body (a cold wind inside his head, behind his eyes), this momentary oblivion of the leaden mass of skull on neck, he would have refused to believe it. That was denied him, had to be denied him; if not, why had he so feared that he would never find her, why had he cried in the mornings, while the kettle boiled, and why had he enjoyed punishing himself by placing the childish whimpering of his eyelids in the path of the steam when he opened the teapot? This woman had arrived so that would no longer happen. He knew it from the first time he heard her speak—it was a question about the cards, but he had never thought the cards and their movements could interest anyone—because her voice was nothing like his mother's and yet also seemed to have been speaking to him in secret or by stealth since he was a boy. That night, returning to Liège in his van, twice he thought he saw her driving the cars that overtook him, thought he saw her long, black hair like a Bedouin's djellaba, saw on a finger of the hands on the steering wheel of each car a ring identical to the one he'd used to perform in public the oldest trick in the world. And the next morning, while reading in bed after breakfast the last pages of *David Copperfield*, he realized that Mrs. Micawber was no longer gray-haired and fifty, but appeared suddenly young again, carrying a riding whip all the time and keeping her throat wrapped up in a scarf with two embroidered stirrups. The exchange was like an order: Chopin knew that he had to go and see her. Distracted by the emotion of the image, he put the book down on top of the plate stained with egg yolk and began to practice in front of the mirror, as the only way to kill time, the way to make a queen of hearts be replaced by the king in spite of the entire deck separating them. It was a trick he'd been practicing for thirteen days and which would spring to mind a few months later, at the very moment of the accident, as if it were also written that he'd never iron out the final details and that Selma would never be allowed to see it executed perfectly. But he knew none of this that morning, nor the following Thursday, when he went home after making love for the first time with a real woman (so real that she was expecting another man's child), a woman he would protect forever, a woman different from those prostitutes on Rue des Guillemins he'd unburdened himself with before and who now, according to a decision by the municipality of Liège, had begun to pose in illuminated display windows instead of putting on their coats and strolling around the neighborhood, so the puritanical or timid pedestrian who passed by without looking at them, the hand shielding the eyes like a horse's blinders, was forced to step on these suggestive shadows: a torso and a pair of shoulders and the line of a garter belt projected onto the paving stones of the sidewalk, or in the case of a woman as tall as Selma, as far as the curb.

IV

Caroline meant strong and brave, and was also the feminine version of Charles, Selma's father's name; and for a combination of both reasons she insisted on this name, in spite of its vaguely Germanic sounds not being much to her husband's taste. The baby girl was born near the beginning of February, on the tenth, which that year fell on a Sunday and immediately after a heavy snowfall. On the way home, Selma tilted her seat back until all she could see were the electricity cables (at first), the crowns of the oak trees (later), and the woven new wool that was the winter sky (always), and she was grateful that her eyelids closed on their own from the exhaustion of giving birth in spite of three whole days of doing nothing but sleeping and swallowing salted biscuits, a total of four bottles of milk with honey, and all the green apples from the fruit baskets that kept arriving in the room, with bows and cards, while her little girl recovered in a glass case, not crying very much according to the nurse—who did like the name because it was also that of the princess of Monaco—crying nonstop according to that nervous husband who paced back and forth in front of the cribs like a hungry vulture. When she was little, Selma had played a game of lying down on the backseat of her parents' old Studebaker and guessing, from glimpses of treetops or chimney features, which part of the journey they were on, how much longer until they'd be home. This time, how-ever, her fingers were moving, counting: a closed fist and her fingers coming up in turn, one, two, three, because Selma was trying to figure out how long it had been since she'd seen Chopin, how many days it would be prudent to let pass before going to find him. Something palpitated in her womb, and between her legs was a disarray of muscles, a sort of phantom contraction, like the way soldiers (her husband had told her) felt pain in a leg after it had been amputated. But it must be an effect of the delivery, not desire, never of headstrong desire.

Since that autumnal Thursday that Selma had received the magician and taken him to bed, until the day her contrac-tions started, she and Chopin had met every Saturday at nine in the morning, taking advantage of the hunting season and the invitations Léopold received (to Modave, to somewhere near Spa, some farther afield, almost to the French border) to go and kill boars or small deer that would sometimes be cooked in the host's kitchen and served at his house the same night, events Selma would attend with good spirits and better appetite, letting her husband make her comfortable in a nice wicker chair, put his hand on her hair as if she were a sick child, and bring her plates of food and glasses of lemonade, without her having to move even to clean off a little cherry sauce she'd dripped onto her dress. They had decided, as coldly as if it were a judicial concession or a signature on a mortgage, that Chopin would continue coming to see her, he would be the one to drive the twenty minutes (a bit less on empty Saturday roads) from Liège to Ferrières, because the full moon of flesh and skin prevented Selma from getting into a driver's seat without her belly button coming into contact with the padded steering wheel. So it was the magician, whose supernatural sense of time enabled him to do without watches without ever being late, who arrived at the house in the Ardennes when barely forty minutes had passed since Léopold's departure, parked on the other side of the road—in front of the abandoned caravan where a family of Albanian gypsies had lived for a few months—came through the gate looking straight at the dry rectangle left on the gravel, the white space the husband's four-by-four had occupied during the rainy night, and entered the house through the French doors of the kitchen, which Selma unlocked when she came down, just after dawn to put the coffee on the stove. The smell of fresh coffee in the air worked as a secret code on Chopin and at the same time as an arousing drug, and so he climbed the stairs, hands in his pockets (a key ring, a deck of cards), his gaze fixed on the last step like that of a missing person returning, but without hunger or shock, simply wanting to slip into a warm bed and feel protected. Selma, for her part, knew that she had time for a shower after seeing Léopold off, but instead of taking one she undressed under the covers, opened her legs as if she were already in labor, and began to touch herself, her fingers barely caressing her pubic hair and then her inflamed vulva, fondling with fascination all the changes in her vagina. Chopin rapped twice on the door frame before going into the bedroom and immediately hung his jacket on the doorknob, and when he got into bed with Selma he had a curious impression of the fluidity of his body, as if the lover didn't even have to lift the bedclothes to find himself beside her, nuzzling her underarm with his head like a newly hatched baby bird and searching out her lips, the earthen rings of her nipples. Unlike Léopold, he did not fall asleep after ejaculating inside her with his mouth open on her back, salivating, his hips shaking; instead he lay on his side, his head resting on his right hand, and looked at her, but in his gaze there was no realization but a sort of diaphanous blank, as if the orgasm had emptied him also of the ability to identify where he was, the name of the woman whose bed he was sharing. After sex, she filled her bathtub with hot water and delighted in entering that rudimentary void; it was a pleasure to lose the sensation of weight, feel light although round as a bottle, free of the unfriendly gravity that made her ankles ache all day long. Then she called Chopin and asked him to sit on the lid of the toilet and explain how he did one of his tricks, and thus, floating in bathwater up to her neck, breathing in the steam and the delicate scent of the oatmeal soap, facing a magician doing what magicians never do (facing a telltale magician, a traitor to his breed), she felt full and contented, thought there would never be any reason to modify this routine.

Selma and Chopin were able to see each other again on March 28, one month and two weeks after she came back from the hospital to her house in the Ardennes, the time she considered sufficient for the small incision to scar over—the obstetrician had prescribed three months but was undoubtedly taking extra care. Léopold had stopped hunting during that time, and took such zealous care of his wife, and such stoic care of his newborn daughter (he got up at four in the morning and went out into the murderous cold to feed the dog, Sido, distract him, and thus postpone his barking), that Selma was occasionally tinged with guilt and almost pity. To what point did that innocent man know that his consideration was at the same time vigilance, that the care he was lavishing on her was most of all taking care of himself. Selma thought of this on the Friday when, after lying to Léopold about some yellow flowers that she needed to buy in the Place de la Cathédrale (not to be the last to celebrate spring), she dropped him off at his office in Mont-Saint-Martin and crossed Liège heading for Guillemins station, driving slowly because the thaw had made the streets slippery. The hoteliers' lack of imagination struck her as incredible, squandering the opportunity to baptize their businesses with bold or attractive names—were they not, after all, places where bold men and attractive women went to make love?—and preferring to make use of the neighborhood or a cliché, and so a hotel on the banks of the Oise was called Hôtel de l'Oise, and one on the other side of the river was called Hôtel Simenon, in spite of the fact that the writer had never set foot in its premises, and had even died before its construction. And so the Hôtel Guillemins took its name from the nearby station, so nearby that the room rate doubled if the windows did not overlook the incessant rattling and jolting of the trains; but Selma didn't know if the station was named after the prostitutes' street, or the prostitutes' street after the station. She wanted to ask Chopin, but when she found him beside the counter, amusing himself with a telephone book—seeing how many surnames he could memorize before she arrived—all her mouth would do was fall open into a kiss, and the novelty of Chopin's hands closing around her waist and spanning it made her laugh out loud and also made the blood rush up to her cheeks, because she recognized that she'd become indispensable to the man, or at least had been continuously imagined by him during all that time, and the other novelty, the one she'd foreseen in silence, gave her shivers, because once upstairs, after being almost pushed by those avid hands up against the bathroom wall (the neon lights came on and went out and the lovers laughed), after those hands, as nimble and precise as those of a surgeon, showed so much evidence of clumsiness in undressing her and even popped a mother-of-pearl button off the red blouse she'd chosen so carefully, after all that, then, lying down faceup with legs open to the sweaty body and erect member assailing her, showing herself to Chopin as she'd never done before that instant, was something both as shameful and as wild as losing her virginity all over again, and the space between her breasts that smelled of milk and perfume filled with color and her eyes opened and her stretched belly felt contact with the other skin, and Selma knew she'd never forget the way the cold light from the street was changing on this new belly, on these hips widened by the effort of the delivery, on the bright white stretch marks like slimy trails of a cemetery snail.

After the sex, Selma stared at herself perplexed. The light coming in the window had lowered as if the cheap blind were a workman's ladder, and the long, horizontal shadows in the room made her feel even more changed and she wondered when the transformation had actually taken place, where the other half of her life was, because Chopin, now getting dressed on the other side of the bed (his back to her, the hem of his shirt barely revealing his skinny buttocks), suddenly seemed like a place where she could lose herself, the man who had deflowered her and demanded to possess her. For the first time, she had seen his face as he penetrated her, his mouth seeking her nipples, which in the semidarkness looked violet, and that image was the one that threatened to colonize her imagination until all that happened again. That's what she was thinking as she went through the terrible steps that would return her to the real world; however, she did not know, could not know, what was going on inside the magician's head, because Chopin still remained, in spite of everything, as inscrutable as the day he made her wedding band end up on her husband's key ring. And so she was not surprised, as they descended the dark stairs and saw the blurry silhouette of a man framed in the etched glass, when her lover identified him immediately, certain that they were facing Léopold and how futile and perhaps childish it would be to turn around—go back to the room, hide in a closet, slip out the fire escape. What shook her first was a shudder of loss, or anticipation of loss, as looking at Léopold's face she already had her daughter's image in her mind, and knew that she could renounce the magician but not her little girl's chance to grow up in the company of her father.

Léopold greeted Chopin with a handshake that seemed anachronistic and rather affected, something like a slap with a white glove or a message sent through seconds, and asked Selma only where she had parked the jeep and if she minded them, the three of them, discussing this matter at home, so no one would bother them, and so they, the three of them, could make the appropriate decisions, with cool heads, serenely and dispassionately. Selma, of course, could not know how mistaken she was in accepting with that kind of inertia that dragged her (since she was the one who knew where the vehicle was and who had the keys in her bag) to the driver's seat, from which she could but did not want to look at Chopin, sitting in the backseat, and wanted to but could not look at

Léopold, that cruel passenger whose eyes scrutinized her, finding and itemizing the infinite signs of adultery, the flushed blotches at her neck and on her lips, hair messed up at the nape of her neck, the veins on the back of her hand slightly welled up (and on her hand the gleaming ring, silent as a spy). By the time they left Liège it was completely dark, and the amber lights from the dashboard made Selma feel a feverish heat in her hands. On the highway, Chopin disappeared from the rearview mirror; the black waters in the frame were broken only by the headlights of the cars following them. Later Selma would try to recall that instant in general, and in particular what had happened in the backseat of the car she was driving, because it was that brief distraction (the eyes watching the road strayed from it for a moment to find those of her lover) which caused the accident. Leaving the highway, at the exact point where Léopold began to eat his cheese sandwich every morning, something moved under the wheels the way the floor used to move when Selma was pregnant. She slammed on the brakes, honked the horn, but the car kept sliding forward on the frozen drizzle and crashed into the brick wall of a pharmacy. Léopold's head smashed through the windshield: he must have died instantly. In Chopin's head something very different happened.

He saw a queen and a king at opposite ends of a deck of cards. He saw the space a wedding band needed to cross to link onto a key ring. He saw his teacher, Jacques Lambert, put a redheaded woman inside a black box and then turn her into a Bengal tiger. He saw an American magician put, in place of the Statue of Liberty, a void of illuminated fog. His hands moved in response to this sketch of replacements, to order the world he'd disordered, exchanged a live body for a dead one, lifted by the armpits a man whose head was broken and put him in the place of the woman who'd been driving. And only when he'd carried out the swap and knew that Selma was safe, that she wouldn't have to take responsibility for the accident, that no judge could saddle her with negligence or guilt or involuntary manslaughter, Chopin collapsed in his seat with the sensation of having done what was expected of him for the first time in his life. He didn't know if he lost consciousness, because he confused the imaginary audience's applause with hurried steps on the asphalt, and only after waking up did he understand that the shouts of enthusiasm, at his magisterial sleight of hand, were not shouts but Selma crying and screaming and tearing at the painful air.

V

Those who went to the burial at the Aywaille cemetery saw him accepting responsibilities not his to assume. Chopin attended those who wished to say farewell to Léopold and even allowed some to go up to see his widow, who was quietly breaking down in an eddy of bedclothes (tears sprang from her open eyes as if from a mechanical doll) and had brought her daughter's cradle to the side of the bed so she would not stop rocking her for an instant (in the silent icy room, her arm was the only movement). For those present, Chopin was still an employee of the company transformed, by virtue of solidarity or sympathy, into a friend of the family; it was later they learned of his secret life, of the affair, of his role in the accident. By the time the details came to light the lovers had separated, their lives had gone in different directions, one without the other: he to Namur, as an assistant in a whole-food shop and restaurant, and she embedded in her Ferrières house, where she still wakes up in the middle of the night to see her husband standing at the foot of the bed or starting down the stairs as if it's time to get up and put the coffee on. After a few months, when Chopin visited her with the intention of recovering something, of reliving the confusing emotions that had brought him so close to happiness, she received him out of courtesy and spoke of the father, not of the lover, for the length of time it took to empty a teapot. On her lap, or on the blanket as thick as a poncho that covered her from the waist almost to her parallel feet, was a notebook with iridescent covers and a pencil sharpened with a utility blade and tied to the chair with a leather cord. Without lifting the book, Selma told him that she'd started to write down anecdotes about Léopold—his cheese sandwich, what he said before going out hunting—

because she, who had grown up without a father, wished her mother had thought of doing this. It was obvious, from the crossed-out lines and an arrow that ran right over the seam of the book from one page to the other, that her ideas weren't clear, that the memory of her dead husband was already escaping her; but to Chopin, who was beginning to glimpse the undeserved sentence of solitude, this interested him less than the detail of the hanging pencil, a leather pendulum. When he asked her about it, Selma explained that the cord allowed her to find the pencil easily, without wasting time or having to call anybody, when the spasms of fatigue paralyzed the muscles in her hand and forced her to drop it. The hand is a beautiful apparatus, she said then, but still so far from perfect, and pencils are alive and reluctant and sometimes unkind creatures: one tends to drop them, by accident or out of clumsiness or exhaustion, and they can roll for whole kilometers.

Life on Grimsey Island

I

Oliveira didn't really care where the hotel was, because he didn't intend to stay there any longer than necessary. When she was still sober, Agatha had suggested a family-run inn she thought she'd seen near the Auneuil exit, a few months earlier, one day when she'd been called to take care of an old mare with a broken leg. "Putting them down always depresses me," she'd told Oliveira in her tired voice, "that's why I don't take those jobs anymore. The one that day was the last." After a routine procedure with no complications, Agatha had thought a coffee with brandy might make the memory of the mare dying easier to bear—the fearful neighing, the tension in the spotted legs that gave way as the drug advanced toward the heart—and had gone into a place with a silhouette of a jockey with a riding whip and spurs on the sign. The inn was so pleasant, and it was run by such a nice old man, that Agatha had promised to return and spend a night in one of the four rooms upstairs.

"The old man fought in the war," she told Oliveira. "But he deserted to be with his family, and no longer found it humiliating to confess. I congratulated him. I would have done the same."

It soon became obvious they weren't going to find the old deserter's inn: Agatha couldn't remember which route she'd taken that afternoon, and all the streets in the village looked like the same street with recently painted yellow signs and green wooden doors that looked black at night. It was a relief for Oliveira: he'd imagined the old man's effusive greeting—he'd have a luxuriant mustache that would cover his lips—curious to know who Oliveira was and what his relationship was to the woman, whether they wanted a double bed, if they wanted to be woken early. He couldn't help finding the prospect of that sort of affability, that forced familiarity, objectionable.

So they kept driving. They decided to track the arrows, obey the inert instructions, and go to an Etap, one of those automatic hotels for a hundred eighty francs a night where nobody mans the desk after ten, and clients register at a screen and use codes as long as telephone numbers to open the doors of the garage, the building, and the room itself.

"You don't have to talk to anybody," said Oliveira. "Don't have to smile or give any explanations."

"You're ashamed to be seen with me?"

"Of course not, Agatha."

"We could go in separately. I can say I'm your aunt, or something."

"None of that. Don't be ridiculous."

Agatha smiled and closed her eyes.

"How romantic," she teased. "Our first fight."

Then the red wine made her start to doze off, and Oliveira found that, if he pressed down the clutch and took his foot off the accelerator, he could hear her breathing, the light snoring of a stuffed-up little girl. When they arrived, Oliveira stopped the van outside the main entrance—a banner of white light bathed the hood in its vulgar brightness, and a smeared hand-print appeared on the windshield—took his credit card out of his wallet, and before getting out, heard Agatha stir, open her eyes, and say she was delighted they'd chosen such a well-lit place. For him there was something attractive in that giving in to childhood fears on the part of an older woman he'd met a few hours before and with whom he was now looking for a bed where they could make love.

He came back rubbing his hands together. In his lips he held a little piece of paper with serrated edges. Agatha took it from him gently, holding it between her thumb and index finger and waiting for him to open his mouth. The tremor of his door as it banged shut didn't startle her, but shook the empty bottle under her bare feet. Oliveira wished at that moment that he'd had a drink as well, because the wine would have warmed him up.

"It's never been so cold," he said.

"I was dreaming of my daughter," she said. "I dreamed she was alive, here in the back, and we were talking about horses."

"She couldn't have been back there. It's full of cases and bags."

"And my instruments."

"Yes. The heaviest of all."

"Don't exaggerate. But a person could easily fit. The proof is that in the dream all that was there and Alma as well. She was asking me what the syringe was for, the scalpel. In the dream she was wearing a Charleston boa."

"What does the little paper say?"

"Three nine at the beginning," said Agatha, "nine three at the end. A few more numbers in between. Do you want me to go?"

Before he could reply, she was standing, in bare feet and furrowing her brow, in front of the sliding garage door. With two long strides that didn't betray the alcohol levels in her bloodstream she was at the keypad. She reproduced the number—Oliveira could hear the beep each time she pressed a button—and smiled when the white light illuminated the entrance and the door slid along its rail set into the pavement.

Oliveira stepped lightly on the accelerator. There was something familiar in that situation, a certain domestic ease that made it unlike a one-night stand. He opened the window as he passed her: a husband coming home, a man expected somewhere.

"Thanks," he said.

"It's like Ali Baba's cave," said Agatha.

The room was on the second floor. They had to go up a couple of flights of stairs with green carpeting, so worn that their feet barely felt it, and walk down to the end of an ammonia-scented corridor. Only the electric hum of an ice machine broke the silence. When they got to number 17, again she was the one who punched in the code. The tones they found when they entered were violets and fuchsias, the bedspread a lewd purple, the metal bed frame was pink like icing. Beside the bed a half-length mirror reflected a man not as young as Oliveira. He ran his hands over his temples and some loose hairs stuck to them, and he noticed calmly that his forehead had broadened over the last couple of years, like a shoreline during floods.

"Three nine, nine three," she said.

"What about it?"

"It begins with my age and ends with my age."

Oliveira kept his face as straight as a gambler's. He could smell the woman's breath, sour from wine and lipstick.

"But backward, no?"

"Yes, backward," said Agatha. "It would be a palindrome of my age if the numbers in between weren't so disorderly."

Agatha crossed her arms over her waist and took off her blouse without even unbuttoning it, as carefree as someone trying on old clothes in a theater dressing room. Her breasts had white parallel stretch marks like trails of milk. Between the cups of her cotton bra hung a silver cross that Oliveira hadn't seen when they pulled out of the gas station. The Christ, as if made of pearl, seemed stained by lotions, perfumes, and sweat.

"Did I tell you what your surname would be in Iceland?"

Oliveira shook his head, his back to her. He was looking for a hanger in the closet to keep his shirt from getting wrinkled. He couldn't help smiling: a bachelor's habits.

"Franciscosson," said Agatha. "That's what your surname would be. Horrible, don't you think?"

II

He had found her (it was exactly the right verb) at an exhibition of circus horses six kilometers north of Beauvais, on the property the equestrian Francisco Oliveira's heirs, one of whom he had no desire to be, had turned into a fairground. The place was no more than five minutes off the A16, but the willows and the whistling of the wind and the horses kicking in their stalls, or perhaps a combination of it all, warded off the din of traffic like erasing the static on a tape recording. At dusk, when the public had left, Oliveira wanted to take one last look at his father's property, not out of any kind of nostalgia, but in order, later in his life, to be able to describe what he'd given up. There were people in the livery stable. Oliveira circled around the back wall, trying to identify the voices coming from inside without being seen. He peered through the cracks in the wood: there was Antonio, the Portuguese man who'd looked after the stables for the last seven years, accompanied by a woman. Between them, a Lusitanian stallion lowered and raised his head. It could be Elmo, might be Urano. Oliveira never called the horses by their names; he refused to put himself on the same level as them in his father's regard. Urano, Elmo, Oliveira junior: three different forms of the old rider's satisfactions. Was that what Oliveira had been, one more lodger at the stables? As a boy, that question had frequently crossed his mind. Now, about to leave it all behind, he was almost ashamed of remembering those regrets.

He walked around the side of the livery stable and undid the wooden bar latch. The bar fell beside him with a crash that startled the woman. The horse didn't bat an eyelid. Oliveira realized he was sedated.

"Don't stand there gawking," she said. "Come and help us."

"I don't know anything about horses," said Oliveira.

The woman wore a cooking apron that said MON ROYAUME POUR UN CHEVAL. Her hair was the color of a crow's feather, and her angular, sad facial features looked as though they'd been carved with a knife on a bar of soap. She obviously didn't know she was speaking to the son of Francisco Oliveira.

"You know how to hold a bag up in the air," she said.

Oliveira approached. Minutes earlier he'd been walking beside the stream that flows out of the Thérain, and now the sawdust stuck to his shoes and the hems of his jeans. The woman handed him a clear plastic bag half full of a transparent liquid. It wasn't sunny, but the slanted winter light still managed to play with the prism of water in the bag. On Oliveira's wrist and arm it drew red, yellow, and purple figures. From the bag a tube descended and disappeared into the animal's side; they had shaved the area where the needle went in. Oliveira felt the absurd sensation of localized cold, as if only in that space where the flesh was visible the skin bristled. He looked through the bag. He saw the oblong sign on which Francisco Oliveira had summarized his idea of horsemanship: CADENCE, LÉGÈRETÉ, GÉOMÉTRIE. He saw two deformed heads—a soapstone bust that had once been beautiful, black, lively hair—and the huge eyes of a horse beginning to nod off.

"Hold the bag up high," said the woman. "Above your shoulder, at least."

The horse began to wobble. His front legs trembled for an instant, and then his body fell sideways like the façade of a building, raising a cloud of sawdust with the dull thud of his flesh. But he refused to put his head on the floor, and the woman had to kneel on his neck and all her weight was barely able to overcome the patient's resistance. The horse blinked; he panted; his lips hung open like resin revealing the pink gums, the white teeth hard as plaster. Antonio tied a strap around the left hoof and fastened it to the railing of the stands. As he pulled the strap, the horse's legs separated and revealed the genitals, black as oil against the brown of the groin. The woman brushed the dust off the testicles with her bare hands, washed the area with a bile-colored liquid and then with hot water, and an apparition of steam rose in the cold air. She moved her hands in the pail of water—Oliveira noticed the edges dirty with dog food—dried them with a mauve towel that she spread out on top of the sawdust, and on the towel the instruments for the operation. The woman took out of an aluminum case a small scalpel, the size of her little finger, and drew a precise line on the horse's scrotum. It wasn't as if she were cutting: the scalpel was a felt-tip pen and the animal's skin fine paper. But the blade had cut. The scrotum opened like fruit rind, separated as if it had a life of its own, and the smooth white testicles were exposed to the air, luminous against the black skin.

Then the woman made another cut. The first trickle of blood appeared; immediately the white fruit of the testicles was covered in red. The woman squeezed both hands at the base of the scrotum and the testicles popped out. She raised the scalpel and cut something else, but at that moment Oliveira had to kneel down in the sawdust because he felt his head emptying of blood and the world before his eyes turning black.

"What's the matter?" said the woman.

"He's going to faint," said Antonio.

"Stand up, for God's sake. I need that serum flowing."

Oliveira heard them, but had no voice.

"Well, you hold the bag, Antonio. I've almost finished."

Oliveira didn't see her finish. He stayed on his knees, his back to the animal. When he turned around, a sort of masculine shame kept him from looking between the horse's legs: his gaze came to rest on the horseshoes that reflected the darkened sky. In this cleansing space the woman appeared, and Oliveira thought the fatigue in her expression was not the result of the operation, but had been with her for a long time.

"Are you all right?"

"I'll get over it," said Oliveira.

"Do you want to come in? A cup of tea, or something hot, would do you good."

Oliveira shook his head.

"I have to get going."

"But you're not going to drive like that, it's dangerous," the woman said.

Oliveira saw she wasn't smiling: her voice was more pleading than polite.

"Half an hour more, half an hour less," she added. "Wherever it is you're going, it's not going to make any difference."

WHEN OLIVEIRA TOLD HER that all of that, the stables and every mare and every stallion, the livery and the right to use it, the two hectares of arable land surrounding the large house, could have belonged to him and he had renounced it all, Agatha's hands flew to her head and she called him crazy, foolish, deranged. Then Oliveira heard himself explaining his father's life with indifference that wasn't exactly genuine and without too many details—but touching on the subject, even if only in monosyllables and short phrases, was already a rarity—speaking about the man who was the master of equestrian artistry and traveled all over Europe and even as far as Brazil teaching admiring students the art of sitting in a saddle. Agatha had also admired him at some point, and Oliveira couldn't find a way to make her understand his contempt for the world of Lusitanian horses: she would have found it absurd to abandon a place like Beauvais with the arguments that sounded too much like those of an only son jealous of his father's profession, the tantrum of a spoiled little boy. Had it been a simple slight, Oliveira thought, his motives would be easily explicable. But the memory of his father was tainted with resentments, pinned not on a lifetime's assessment but

on precise and painful images. Oliveira did not belong anywhere and that was his father's fault. He had only two or three
memories of his mother, as if he'd concentrated all his energy
on that paternal anthology of reproaches. They'd arrived in
France when he was still a boy. Their route had been the opposite of that of most other immigrants: they began on the
outskirts of Paris and, as they became more secure, as the rider's prestige was recognized in Brussels and Stuttgart, they
moved away from the capital and out to the provinces. Oliveira
grew up with the notion of living in a foreign country, but
knowing that none belonged to him. He earnestly pretended
whenever faced with a flag. He envied other children who
used French without feeling clumsy. Gradually he noticed, little by little, he was forgetting his own language.

He could have told the woman about these memories and
said: "This house is my father, these horses are my father.
Now do you understand why I'm leaving?" But he didn't. He
concentrated on practical questions, the total area of the property, the price of the stallions. When his father died, the estate
was divided up easily and in less than three weeks, so many
people were due a share of the inheritance if the son turned it
down. The only condition Oliveira imposed was that Antonio
should keep his job, but that didn't keep the foreman from
telling him what was in his head. "One doesn't throw a life
away just like that, kid. One would have to be sick at heart.

You act as if you've lived alone your whole life, as if no one's ever loved you." But Oliveira went ahead, without thinking that selling the property, instead of renouncing it, would have at least gotten him some money, which he was going to need. The compensation he'd received, not for the place but for the purebred his father had given him for his twenty-first birthday, was all the money Oliveira had now.

"I spend my life taking care of horses, and you get rid of them," said the woman. "Incredible that we're sitting here together."

"Don't you ride?"

"Only very badly," she said.

They were sitting on one of the long wooden benches in the kitchen, beside the gas stove, trying to warm up a little. The lamp over the sink cast a bright yellowish light around the room, and the stove projected an ostrich-shaped shadow. Oliveira realized that it had been a long time since he'd last exchanged more than a couple of polite phrases with a woman: gratitude for merits not his own but his father's, promises to keep in touch and organize something with the Beauvais horses at the next festival. Perhaps for this reason he thought it lucky that Agatha had arrived in town by train, that someone else—a gay journalist with a German accent—had given her a lift from the station. Now he, who was heading south, could drive her home to L'Isle-Adam, which was barely out of his way. He suggested it, and the ease with which she accepted allowed Oliveira to consider her vulnerable and fantasize from that moment on about her body and the infinite possibilities that might result from a man and a woman traveling alone between the towns of the Oise, each of them alone but traveling together, with the awareness that a night of sex wouldn't transform them but might be, as had happened to him with other women for one night, an anesthetic, numbing his solitude.

They left about nine, when the December night had fully settled in. Oliveira's van was parked under an oak tree; the air vents and the windshield wiper blades were covered with twigs and wet leaves. Agatha saw the logo of the rental company, green and yellow letters slanted as if caught in the wind.

"Oh, but you're really leaving entirely," she said. "I didn't realize things were so serious."

He spoke to himself.

"Of course I'm leaving entirely," he said. "I don't imagine there's any other way to leave."

After packing, Oliveira had realized that five cubic meters was quite a bit more than he needed. The blonde at the agency had warned him, of course, but Oliveira couldn't manage to persuade himself that her face—her upper lip covered in a yellow scab as if she were just getting over a nasty flu—inspired confidence. So, in the cargo compartment, the luggage Oliveira was beginning his journey with took up a little more than half the available space: two garbage bags full of clothes and several cardboard boxes left enough room for a person. Agatha read: HAUT-PLANTADE, THIERRY GROS CAILLOUX, HAUTS-CONSEILLANTS.

"They're all wine boxes," said Agatha.

"Yes, but only one has bottles in it. The rest are full of records and cassettes, movie magazines. Things like that."

"Any photos?"

"Photos of what?"

"I don't know, the maestro, some horse. Is there no part of this house you might want to remember some day?"

Oliveira thought it over or pretended to.

"No, none," he said finally. "Do you have photos of your family?"

"Only of Alma. My daughter. But that's because she died two years ago, and I don't want to forget what she looked like."

Oliveira was going to say he was sorry: *I'm very sorry to hear that* or *My deepest condolences*, but both phrases seemed awkward, ill-suited to the casualness of the revelation, and he couldn't think of any others.

"Tell me more," he said then. "We've only talked about me. Tell me what your partner does, for example."

"He's long gone. He left when Alma was a zygote."

Oliveira was shaken by the force of her cynicism. He felt indiscreet: that's what you get for trying to approach a stranger.

Agatha kept talking, seeming at ease. She leaned back toward the load with a cat's curiosity.

"Which is the box of wine?" she said. "I feel like a drink, maybe that would warm us up."

Then they took the N1 south, a bottle of Saint-Julien held like a baby's bottle between Agatha's feet. By the time the van merged with the heavy traffic of the A16, the surface of the wine was below the top of the label. The rainy season was late in coming; the sky seemed clogged up, invariably gray. Soon the highway was no longer illuminated, and all Oliveira saw was the glare of the lights of northbound cars, that sort of permanent eclipse behind sheets of zinc that separated their lanes from oncoming traffic. Agatha slid down in her seat, took off her shoes with one hand, and put her feet up against the glove compartment. Then she turned on the heating. It blasted Oliveira in the face.

"Sorry. Do you want a sip?"

"Not for me, thanks."

"Very good," she congratulated him. "One does not drink at the helm, everyone knows that."

After passing under a concrete bridge—a fluorescent sign ordered FAITES LA PAUSE TOUTES LES DEUX HEURES—Oliveira slowed down. He changed into the right-hand lane; Agatha asked him if they were going to stop for something as he pulled into a rest area, a concrete bay surrounded by pines. "I just need to use the rest room," he lied. The noise of a fight came out of a bus parked a few meters away. Two teenagers were rolling around on the ground, and the sound of a fist as it thumped into a skull seemed exotic to Oliveira, something forgotten, a childhood memory. "I won't be long," he said as he got out. This, however, was true: he crossed the parking bay toward the services hut, found a tin vending machine built into the wall, put in ten francs, and a little pack of condoms, square and perfect as if no one had ever touched it, dropped into the palm of his hand. The dispenser also offered tooth-brushes and razors. Oliveira decided he wasn't in need of any-thing else and returned to the van.

Agatha had finished the bottle. Her raincoat was hanging over the hand brake, between the two seats. When she spoke, it was clear her tongue was beginning to get tangled up.

"Do you like me, Oliveira?"

He didn't answer.

"Are we going to make love? Because I'd rather not go to my house, that's the only thing."

"Well, let's go somewhere else, then," Oliveira heard him-self say.

He waited a moment and added:

"That is unless you're in any hurry, of course."

"None at all," said Agatha, lowering her head. "It's winter and the fucking night never ends."

III

The television was a luminous window hanging in the corner attached to the wall, and the slanted view Oliveira had from the bed was that of a man with thick glasses standing beside a map of France, indicating with a pointer the route of some electronic clouds across the western half of the hexagon. He was moving his lips but not saying anything, because underneath France, between Nice and Marseille, the word *Mute* ordered his silence. Then a series of squares appeared, Sunday, Monday, Tuesday, Wednesday, and Oliveira saw that he'd have nothing but bad weather for the whole trip, but thought he might reach Clermont-Ferrand ahead of the rain they were forecasting. Who was that man? Why was Martine Desailly not there, the woman who'd been in charge of predicting the weather for years? The one-o'clock news was part of Oliveira's routine, and his day incomplete without the most recent scandal from the Assemblée Nationale or the images of the dead in Algiers, more or less sophisticated forms of violence that vindicated his desire to leave, to hide away from the world. Agatha was sleeping. After sex, she had locked herself in the bathroom for fifteen minutes; Oliveira was going to ask if she was feeling all right, but then saw that she hadn't redone her makeup, as he'd thought at first, but that the dampness of her eyes was displacing her mascara a little. He thought it would be futile to ask her why she'd been crying, when they were going to say good-bye in an hour and never see each other again in their lives. He felt cynical but also justified in refusing to accumulate other people's sadness when it wasn't within his power to alleviate it. "I'm going to sleep for a little while, if you don't mind," Agatha had said, "but don't be embarrassed about waking me up if we have to get going."

"Don't worry, have a good sleep," said Oliveira. "Shall I turn off the light?"

"No. Leave it on."

"I don't mind turning it off. So you can sleep better."

"It's fine as it is, Franciscosson. Leave it on."

Oliveira saw her move one hand over her forehead and chest in a quick blessing degenerated from use, like a businessman's signature. Agatha, with her eyes already closed, kissed the Christ on her necklace and rolled over.

Now, Oliveira watched her sleep. He did not envy her turbulent sleep; the woman's body frequently shook as if she were falling through the air in her dreams. Her constant little kicks had uncovered her: her hips had the marks of someone who had lost weight quickly—perhaps after pregnancy, Oliveira already knew that her daughter was dead but didn't want to know more—and on her thighs the dimpling of cellulite gave her skin the look of fine cork. The hair on her body glistened with the changeable halo of the television like synthetic thread, like the nylon line on a fishing rod. Oliveira went around the other side of the bed, knelt down on the carpet, his gaze at the level of her barely visible vulva. This woman had been beautiful, that was obvious; Oliveira had been aroused by her innocence in bed, her apparent docility, her reluctance when he suggested she turn over.

Then she seemed to sense Oliveira's gaze.

"What's up? Do we have to get going?"

He hadn't thought of that, but he looked at his watch. He still had to take Agatha home and find a rest area, perhaps on the other side of Paris, to get a little sleep before dawn, so he wouldn't be nodding off on the drive south. Ever since he'd decided to leave he'd found himself in moments like this, when it seemed like his arrival was something illusory, something that would never happen.

"Yes, it's time," said Oliveira. "Shall I hand you your clothes?"

The woman sat up in bed. Her breasts dropped slightly, not scrawny but full like bags, like the bag of serum Oliveira had held that afternoon.

"Well, then," Agatha grumbled like a girl getting up for school. "If we have to go, we have to go. Of course, I haven't got a vote on this."

Outside, an icy wind bit their ears and dried their lips. As soon as they stepped into the garage, a motion detector switched on a bright light. Her shadow gathered in on itself, a shapeless, inhuman silhouette.

"So," said Oliveira. "Tell me how to get to your house."

"My house," Agatha repeated in irritation. "You know what? If it were up to me, I'd stay here until morning."

"Well, stay. What's the problem?"

"The problem is that France is not covered in railway lines, monsieur. Or perhaps you've seen a train going by here? And with the price of a taxi I could pay for five nights in a hotel like this."

"Exactly," said Oliveira. "That's why I'm going to drive you, that's why I need to know how to get there."

Agatha didn't say anything.

"How do you get there?" Oliveira insisted impatiently.

"Yeah, yeah, don't badger me," said Agatha. "Just follow the signs for Paris, that's all. You'll see L'Isle-Adam soon enough, it's pretty straightforward."

This time, however, there was no traffic. Every once in a while, a pair of red lights would whistle past in the left-hand lane and disappear as quickly as they'd appeared; occasionally the van would overtake a transport truck, the bodywork jostling and the steering wheel trembling in Oliveira's hands as he pulled out of the slipstream. Agatha was silent, as if Oliveira had offended her by saying they had to leave the hotel. To make up for the mistake he couldn't quite identify, out of cordiality to a woman he'd slept with or simple pity, pity for the sadness Agatha seemed to carry with her like a snail's shell, Oliveira tried to start up a spontaneous conversation.

What would his name be in Iceland? What had she said he'd be called?

"Franciscosson. The son of Francisco. Francisco, your father, the great Portuguese rider of this century."

"And you?"

"Me what?"

"What would your surname be?"

"Ah." Agatha straightened up in her seat. "Well, my father's name was Raymond, so I would be called Raymonddóttir. The daughter of Raymond. But the two letters together, the *d* of *Raymond* and the *d* of *dóttir*, sound ugly and grating."

"Yes, a little," Oliveira admitted.

"It would have to be Raymondóttir, with just one *d*."

"Doesn't sound that great, either."

"No. Good thing I'm not Icelandic."

Oliveira smiled. Suddenly seeing her like that, lighthearted and carefree, pleased him as if the well-being of this stranger had begun to matter to him.

"Have you been there?"

"No. But I'd like to, God knows I'd really like to. It must be a lovely country, don't you think? Do you know how to say 'I'm lost' in Icelandic? *Ég er týnd*."

"*Eg er tynd*," Oliveira tried to repeat.

One of Agatha's hands moved to her chest; through the material of her blouse her fingers closed over the Christ figure.

"God knows I'd like to live there. Maybe one day I'll be

able to. The night hardly lasts at all, Oliveira. In June, dawn breaks at three in the morning, and night doesn't fall until twelve. And anyway, the sky never darkens completely, it stays as blue as the sea, it never gets this repugnant black we have here."

"But that's in June," said Oliveira. "In winter it must be worse than here."

Agatha wasn't listening. She wasn't looking at him, wasn't looking ahead. Her gaze was lost in some distant point, far beyond the window at her side, a point lost among the grain silos, the fields of crops combed by the wind in yellow waves that were the color of fool's gold against the backdrop of the sky.

"There is an island, in the north of Iceland. It's called Grímsey. The Arctic Circle goes right across the middle of it, cutting it in two. On Grímsey the sun never sets. It's light at midnight, it's light at three in the morning. Can you imagine, Oliveira? A never-ending day, that's there all the time."

"Yes, but that's in the summer. In the winter it must be the opposite, night all the time."

"Light at midnight," said Agatha. "Light at three in the morning. So no one is afraid, no one feels the horror of having a fear of the dark."

The first sign announcing L'Isle-Adam appeared an hour later. Oliveira exited the highway onto one of those minor side roads that always fascinated him because anything could happen along them: a cow, a couple in conversation sitting at the edge of the pavement, and maybe, at the right time of year, a deer leaping across the road.

"Now what do I do?" said Oliveira.

"Straight ahead. I'll tell you, don't worry."

Oliveira looked in the mirror: it had happened. The attack, the urgent need to drop her off and turn back into himself, a man who only counted on himself, a solitary man. And what if she asked him to spend the night with her, to sleep over at her house? He would decline, of course, but how? It was incredible that it still took so much effort to make all the arrangements to conserve his independence, speak those words, make those gestures. It was incredible that life had so insistently proved the futility of any opening up, the greater wisdom of closing in on himself, and he still didn't know how to apply those lessons. He began to think how he'd say good-bye to her, and the evaluation of various displays of affection, a kiss on the lips, cheek, or forehead, an exchange of phone numbers—but he didn't yet have a house to call his own, much less a phone number—seemed to him too much like a children's game. A sign, this time white, announced the entrance to the town on the left, a hundred meters ahead.

"Do I turn here?"

"Yes," said Agatha.

Oliveira looked in the rearview mirror, pushed down the indicator. The van was beginning to turn when Agatha said:

"No, sorry. Keep going straight, it's further on."

A swerve of the steering wheel straightened out the van.

"You sure?"

"I'm a bit sleepy, or still drunk, I don't know. It's straight on, Oliveira."

He obeyed. Agatha refocused her attention, her eyes wide open, scanning the view. *You don't know where you live,* thought Oliveira, *you're lost or don't want to arrive,* and suddenly felt a new link to her: *You hate your house, too.* He went over in his head the times the odometer had clicked around, one, two, three, four, this was a considerable detour, this woman was considerably lost. They crossed Pontoise along a narrow sleeping street plagued with speed bumps that shook the aluminum instrument case like a maraca. Oliveira expected a comment from Agatha, but, although she didn't take her eyes off the road, and although her fingers were crickets that leaped as they recognized the way, nothing came out. They had to get close to Meulan before Oliveira started to understand.

"We're not going to your house, are we?"

Jokingly, she reproached him for being so masculine that he couldn't tolerate losing total and absolute control of the vehicle.

"Agatha."

"What?"

"Where are you taking me?"

"Relax. We're here anyway, we can't turn back now."

She pointed to an embankment leading to an oak-lined drive.

"Turn in," she said.

The gravel shifted under the tires. The house Oliveira arrived at was a façade with no sign of depth, black and flat like a canvas painted to conceal the construction behind it. There were no lights on. From outside, the attic could be seen standing out against the sky.

"Park here," said Agatha, and her thin fingers moved in the air. "Don't turn off the engine, so the lights will shine into the room."

"Aren't there any lights?" Suddenly Oliveira was furious. "But where the fuck are we?"

"My daughter died here," said Agatha. "You'll think I'm crazy, but I wanted you to see the place. I don't know why you, Oliveira, maybe just because you're the one who's with me tonight. Sometimes things are that simple."

TANGLED IN THE BUSHES along the drive were pieces of the police tape they'd used to cordon off the house. Agatha walked ahead and he followed her, breathing the swampy air the autumn rains had produced, the smell of the stagnant water and rotting wood. Oliveira imagined the place next summer, mosquitoes spiraling above the long grass. They walked around the redbrick walls to the glass door into the kitchen. The windows were intact, but the interior was invisible. Agatha turned the knob and the door opened soundlessly. Inside the colors were no different, the world was blue and black.

"They lived here," said Agatha. "Alma spent her last year here, Oliveira."

On the large table with a synthetic cover rested three coffee cups, each on top of a different coaster. One of them had the label of a Belgian brand of beer, Judas. The letters of the word were red, but in the darkness, broken only by the van lights shining through the big front window, the red turned purple as if they were at the bottom of the sea or like the lips of someone who'd frozen to death. Oliveira went into the front room looking all around—not a stick of furniture, no rug, just a parquet floor dulled by dust—scrutinizing the bare, white walls, lacking even a nail hole, that basic trace of humanity, evidence that someone had wanted to take possession of a place with the simple gesture of hanging up an image. He wondered in which of the corners of the house Alma had lain down to die, which room and which bed had been chosen by the person who'd injected her with the morphine Agatha was now mentioning, talking about the autopsy, the communiqué the police had sent out to the close family members of the dead people with the description of the bodies neatly organized, laid out methodically with the rigidity of a military barracks, and covered with a freshly washed white sheet, a terrible quotidian detail as if an affectionate grandmother had just embroidered it for that purpose.

"There were twenty-one bodies," said Agatha. "Most of them were lying on the floor, there, not on the parquet but on mats."

Oliveira tried to conjure up the image.

"As if they were asleep. Each one on their mat, each mat parallel to the next and all of them equidistant from each other."

"How old was your daughter?"

"Seventeen, Oliveira. Seventeen fucking years old. People should have to be old enough to buy booze before they're allowed to join a cult."

It was too sad an irony to be convincing. Oliveira looked outside, the van's lights dazzled him and he felt a sharp pain in his retina. The running engine's murmur reached them, dimmed and distant: the ventilation switched on, the fan belt squealed like an injured animal. Beside the stairs, before going up, Agatha pointed to a niche, the only interruption of the smooth surface of the wall, where the group had kept a nickel silver chalice that was later melted down and a hardcover Bible with rice-paper pages and a velvet bookmark.

"I was able to see it once," said Agatha. "The Battle of Armageddon had been underlined with a light pencil. 'And the armies which were in heaven followed him upon white horses,

clothed in fine linen, white and clean.' That part was underlined, I remember because Alma recited it on a recording she
made for me."

"Light pencil?"

"Yes, you know. Soft lead, or whatever they're called. The
ones architects use."

Oliveira was struck by the way she was talking about it as
if it were a modern relic or a juvenile cult object, Lennon's
glasses or Bogart's hat. When he wanted to tell her, he felt ar-
rogant. Who was he to describe the shape of her grief? The
stairwell smelled of damp and dust, and Oliveira's nose felt
relief when they got to the upper floor, where the air was no
less heavy but had a bit more freedom of movement. The light,
upstairs, was indirect: again blue, again black.

"Do you want me to go down and move the car? If I back
it up a little, maybe we'll get a bit more light."

"No, stay here. The tour's almost finished."

"You don't have to be sarcastic, Agatha."

"Believe me, I do, my dear. It's absolutely necessary."

In the first room on the left, the door was half closed.
Agatha pushed it as if afraid she might wake someone. On
each side of the window was a bunk bed without any ladders.

"They look like the ones in the hotel," said Oliveira. "Except for the color."

"Except they're for sleeping and nothing else," said Agatha.
"Nobody kissed anybody here. They all loved each other but

didn't sleep together. They were committed to God the father, married to their new Church."

She pointed to the bed on the right.

"Alma slept in that one. The four people in this room were women."

Agatha brushed off the dust and sat down on the bare mattress. Oliveira asked:

"Did she sleep on the top bunk or the bottom?"

"Top. She was taller than me, since she was twelve or thirteen she was a head taller than me."

"So why are you sitting down there, then? Come on, I'll help you up."

Agatha stepped into Oliveira's interlaced hands: he lifted her easily, and then steadied her with a hand on her bum. She smiled.

"Cheeky," she said. "You're not coming up?"

Oliveira stretched out on the lower bunk.

"I'm fine here, thanks."

He could feel every knot and every seam of the mattress in his back. He crossed his arms behind his head and closed his eyes. He played at opening them and closing them, acknowledged there wasn't much difference and, nevertheless, that his eyes were adjusting to the dark, and gradually details of the room were coming into focus: the geometric designs carved on the white door, the bare wire hanging from the ceiling where once a lightbulb would have hung. Above his body, the bedsprings creaked with Agatha's every movement. Lying there he realized he couldn't imagine a day of devotion; everything religious was so abstract to him that it was impossible to relate it to waking up, coffee brewing in the kitchen, or taking turns to use the shower. He'd had faith when he was little, of course, because a child is capable of seeing the fulfillment of a prayer, the answer to a plea in anything. And later, what had happened? He got used to the idea of himself, learned that every man is an island, and then the notion disappeared: the notion of that Christian god he'd been told about, that god Oliveira had never seen or heard.

"Oliveira."

"What's up?"

"Nothing. Just wondering if you'd fallen asleep."

"I'm wide awake," he said. He heard the sound of friction. He guessed that Agatha was scratching the wall with her fingernail.

"You wouldn't leave without telling me, would you?" she said.

"I'm quite comfortable here, why would I leave?" said Oliveira. "And you? Do you want to get going?"

There was no answer. Oliveira watched the silvery springs working, the delicate contractions each time the woman above him moved. The nail scraped the wall.

"Sometimes babies suddenly forget to breathe. I don't know why that happens," said Agatha.

And she kept talking. In the days after giving birth, Agatha woke up often in the middle of the night wondering if the little girl was still alive, if she hadn't died. "As happens to babies, Oliveira, you know." Then she'd tiptoe over to the crib and put her face up close to the little girl's: a baby's breathing was one of the quietest things in the world. At that moment, she'd give thanks, thanks to God, sure that no one else was responsible that something as frail as a baby could survive overnight.

"In films there's always someone who wakes up because they feel that someone else is watching them. But it's not a lie, you know."

One night—Alma would have been about twelve, she'd just started her first period—Agatha woke up to find her daughter standing in front of her. She asked her if something was wrong; she imagined first of all what seemed obvious, and told her it didn't matter if she'd stained the sheets. Alma kissed her on the forehead, replied that it wasn't that, and went back to bed.

"It took me almost a year to understand those visits," said Agatha.

Oliveira waited for her to follow up with an explanation, but Agatha fell silent.

"What was it?" he said then. "What did you understand?"

"Alma hadn't stained the sheets," said Agatha. "She never

had nightmares, or any of that nonsense. She simply wanted to make sure I was still breathing."

Then she fell silent.

"And what does that mean, according to you?" Oliveira asked.

But Agatha kept quiet again.

"Don't get all mystical, okay?" said Oliveira in irritation. "There's nothing that annoys me more. We'd better talk about something else. The van, which is still running. If the battery doesn't die, we're going to run out of gas."

"How long till daybreak?"

"Not long, I think. Try to see your watch in this gloom, if you can."

He, however, consulted the sky. He strained to see, tried to concentrate as if his willpower were capable of projecting the violet glints of dawn onto the clouds. A solitary lizard clung to the wall above the window frame, and Oliveira thought that winter would soon kill it.

"I can't see anything. Not a single light anywhere."

"Shit," said Agatha. "Don't leave me alone, okay?"

"I'm not going to leave you alone."

"How can it be dark for so long? Doesn't it seem horrible to you, Oliveira? A person alone, at night. It's like a conspiracy, as if someone did it on purpose, and I swear I'm getting tired of it. It's no life for normal people, is it?"

Oliveira didn't say anything.

"In Iceland it wouldn't be like this. Sometimes I wonder what life would be like on Grímsey Island. It must be different. The sun shining all the time, and you could be outside, doing things. Not thinking. Talking to people, and in daylight, what more could you ask for? Thinking is horrible, all those ghosts, what you've done, what you haven't done. *Góða nótt*, Oliveira, that's good night in Icelandic. But on Grímsey Island they must not even have the chance to say it. Isn't that a perfect life?"

IV

Oliveira drove thinking about the strange way the town had been gradually surrounding them, arranging well-chosen elements on both sides of the road. First a vineyard, then a couple of brick houses, then traffic lights—one green and bright for Paris, Amiens, or Rouen, then another, white and smaller, which didn't direct them toward L'Isle-Adam but confirmed they were in it—and finally, constructed block by block around the van as it advanced along a decidedly urban street. Only one window had a light in it: it was the shop window of a bakery that spilled a yellow light across the sidewalk and part of the road. A man was sweeping the sidewalk with a straw broom; several dry leaves and an Orangina can ended up in the gutter. The letters were projected onto the pavement backward. "Eiregnaluob," said Oliveira. "Boulangerie." He was starting to get sleepy; he felt pins and needles in his hands, found it hard to focus. He looked in the rearview mirror, and saw tiny paths of blood in his eyes like a route map.

"Eiregnaluob," he said.

"What did you say?" she reacted.

"Here we are," Oliveira said.

He parked right in front of the house. At this hour nobody was going to complain: not a single bicycle was visible. As he got out of the van, he felt in his nostrils and tear ducts the cutting cold of the early morning. She seemed more awake; it was as if she'd gotten a second wind. But, in spite of her alert step and clear diction, she was worn-out, no longer the woman whose skillful hands had operated on a horse on the sawdust floor of the Beauvais livery.

While Oliveira was looking for the key to the back doors of the van, she said:

"If you want, you can come in."

Oliveira waited for her to say something more: a romantic proposal, a declared project. Something to flee from.

"It's not something I usually do," she went on. "Well, I never do. If you're not able to take it the right way, forget it and be on your way."

"Take it the right way? What do you mean?"

"As a way of saying thank you."

"But there's nothing . . . but I haven't done anything any other person wouldn't have done."

"That any other person *hasn't* done. But it doesn't matter to you. How I spend my nights is something that doesn't matter to you. What I decide to do—"

"It would give me great pleasure," said Oliveira.

"What would?"

"To see inside your life."

"It's not my life, it's my house," said Agatha. "And it's a mess."

She took her instrument case, and Oliveira followed her inside the house. As soon as he closed the door, he found a living room on the right and a dark wooden handrail going up and a narrow hallway that went all the way to the back, where he could see a wall of sky-blue tiles and the black iron burners of a gas stove. On the widest wall of the front room, above the main radiator, hung a faded map of the world.

"There's no coffee," said Agatha.

"I didn't feel like any," Oliveira lied.

Oliveira was going to say: *Actually, I'm not going to stay very long.* But the heating was so pleasant, the possibility of lying down and closing his eyes for a few minutes so tempting, that the words didn't take shape in his mouth. He could just as easily sleep in a rest area, somewhere along the highway; but here he wouldn't have to worry about thieves or noisy drunks, much less overly sociable creatures trying to look for company, something he, in particular, would be unable to provide. He discovered Agatha's house smelled like her; or, vice versa, that all of her, her underarms, the nape of her neck, her belly button, had been impregnated with this smell, a blend of mothballs and pressed flowers. That, perhaps, gave him the sensation of already knowing or finding himself back in a place he was used to. They went up to Agatha's bedroom, Oliveira's eyes fixed on her hips. He noticed he was desiring her again. Or maybe he was confusing desire with the sudden instinct of belonging.

"I would, however, like to take a shower," said Oliveira. "I'm falling asleep."

"Well, we're in luck, then. That's the only thing I can offer you, hot water."

"You're not so bad," he said, a yawn hindering his words. "You've had a couple of naps."

She didn't hear him.

"Look, this wardrobe is a hundred and eighty years old. It belonged to my great-grandfather's uncle, or something like that. A deacon, in any case."

Agatha's room was not that of a woman who spends much time at home: apart from the wardrobe, a reporter's tape recorder, sitting on top of the television set, was the only proof of human presence. There was nothing to suggest the inhabitant's tastes or opinions. The television was unplugged. Two black cables hung down like lianas and one of them touched the floor. The screen still had the factory adhesive on it, in spite of being an old model. The adhesive was covered in dust. Solitary people like him put the television in their bedroom; lonely, sad people like Agatha soon forgot about the television, left it to rot like fruit.

"This wardrobe is the first Christian of the house," said Agatha.

When Oliveira didn't make any comment, she turned her back on him, as if she were going to inform on someone and ashamed of her duplicity.

"It's all I've got, Oliveira. This shitty religion is all I've got, this God is all that keeps me company, and not you or anyone else can understand that."

"Maybe so. But tonight I've been here. And He hasn't."

"You're leaving."

"And He's staying, is He? Where is He, then? Show Him to me. I've always wanted to meet Him."

"It's all I've got," Agatha repeated. "And you're leaving, Oliveira. Really, it's as if you'd already gone."

"Well, it would be best not to get any hopes up. I was never planning to stay."

"Without pity, please. Have some respect."

"I didn't come here to save you, Agatha."

She closed her eyes. It seemed as though she would rather not have heard the last sentence, but, at the same time, she seemed accustomed to grappling with it.

"It hurts me to think of you leaving. Is that bad? I prefer to convince myself you'll stay until daybreak. I don't suppose that's a sin, carrying on believing things even when you know they're lies."

He didn't dare try to comfort her, much less contradict her. He was afraid Agatha would start to cry, although it was obvious her declaration wasn't intended to provoke sympathy or pity. Maybe, he thought, it wasn't even directed at him, and just a part of this woman's eternal struggle against herself. Nevertheless, he felt cruel. Then he understood he was content, because now he would have liked to erase those words that had threatened the fragile delicacy of the moment.

"Forgive me," he said. "I'm not used to talking about things like this. I don't know how to say what I think without trying to win an argument. It's terrible, my father always scolded me for it."

Agatha took a pair of unpadded headphones out of the wardrobe. "I wanted to show you something," she said. She plugged the headphones into the tape recorder and put them on Oliveira like a princess's tiara.

"Is that a good volume?"

Okay, now a few little things I want you to do for me.

Give my clothes to Father Michel. He knows a Red Cross center nearby that'll take them for sure, and I imagine they'll be use-

ful to some immigrants. I don't know why I didn't ask you this before. Tell him that I looked for the place once to give them the clothes personally, but couldn't find it and ended up lost in Marines. I know you argued with him recently, he told me because I sometimes ask him for advice, and our conversations are long and focused. But don't turn him away, Mama, for your own good. He's not hounding you, like you said, it's not that he wants to force you into anything, he's worried about your soul. He didn't even tell me you don't go to church anymore. I figured it out myself from the things you've told me on the phone.

Everything to do with school you can give to Madame Mabilat, I don't know if some of it might be useful to younger students. Ask her if she remembers the time, when I was in troisième, *that she punished me for spraying yogurt around her desk and crumbling a slice of orange cake on it. Tell her that I dreamed of her furious face recently, but in the dream there was a chicken coop behind the school and I was going to break freshly laid eggs as revenge for the punishment. Ask her if she knows what that means.*

We eat well here, Mama, so don't worry about that. You ask me to tell you how things are, but what you want are material details and I find it very hard to talk about that. I've tried to explain and it's as if you don't hear me, here one distances oneself from all of that, other things matter more. I'm very glad to hear your work with horses is going so well, don't get me wrong. The last time we spoke you told me about the things you'd done, you said the previous Sunday you'd been to a Lusitanian horse fair in Brussels and had a lovely time and forgot for at least a day that I was not at home anymore. And that's when I realized you didn't go to church. I don't have any proof or anything, because I wasn't with you, but I'm still sure you didn't go to church that Sunday. Now do you understand why I chose to be here, with my brothers? Not that I think your influence was negative, of course. I know you're still a good Christian, but I was afraid of straying from our Lord and from the truth in which you educated me. The Lord knows I love you and I admire you, and He has put this congregation in my path so my faith won't be weakened. Always remember it's you who I owe for the discovery of faith.

Last of all: don't keep asking me where we are, understand that our life is now far from our families. Master Albert wants us to gradually detach ourselves from our mortal and earthly pasts, and in a little while I won't be able to send you any more recordings, because we are going on a journey. It has to be enough for you to know there is a light guiding us, and that Christ has died so that light won't go out, so we all have the chance to be born again.

If you see Tempo, give him something to eat from me. He likes raisins and to have his back legs stroked. But don't let him come in 'cause the baker has spoiled him. He gets scared when he's in other people's houses and he might pee, it happened to me once, on the stairs, almost at the top. But I cleaned it up before you got back, and I bet you never even noticed.

OLIVEIRA LOOKED UP and found Agatha sitting on the edge of the bed, naked. She'd opened the heavy curtains, and the vague hint of dawn bathed her flesh in blue, turned her into a specter. Oliveira knew: something was expected of him. But he was as afraid of his reaction fulfilling the woman's expectations as of getting it completely wrong. The world seemed like an impenetrable space at that moment, a room without doors where the luckiest ones walked around wearing blindfolds. He didn't know what to do. He had one certainty: his presence was enough to tow Agatha and bring her to safety, to get her as far as the edge of the night, and that thought touched him with strange pride. Suddenly, nothing was more important. He lay down on his side, his face a few inches away from the buttocks of the seated woman, and he saw how in that position the shadows of cellulite were accentuated. He took her by the shoulder and pulled her toward the pillow, and saw her disappear into the hollow of his underarm like a bird. He felt his fatigue closing his eyelids; he thought if he closed his eyes he'd sleep for three days and not even the outbreak of war would wake him.

"All the parents are wondering the same thing," he heard himself say. "What did they do and what could they have done differently. And this would have happened anyway."

Agatha didn't move. From some point lost in Oliveira's side

came a tiny voice in which there was no complaint or griev-
ance, just a terrible emptiness, the exhaustion of a defeated
person and the notion that this defeat would be repeated until
infinity.

"Before, I needed that, Oliveira. I wanted people to tell me
it wasn't my fault. Now all I want is not to be alone at night.
And in this house I am always alone and now there's no way
to change that."

"That's not true. Everything changes, you just have to
know how to look at it."

"I hate that wardrobe. I hate the deacon, whoever he was,
I hate this house. I hate God, Oliveira."

Oliveira looked up. The ceiling was white plaster; in the
center, an eighteenth-century design had been sculpted without too much talent in bas-relief, unevenly and asymmetri-
cally. "If only I could at least have chosen so many things,"
said Agatha. The hanging lamp seemed to have sickened with
pallor; just as happened at dusk, this moment when the electric light got confused with the gray of the sky was, absurdly,
the darkest of all.

"Dawn is breaking," said Oliveira. "Now you can forget
about Iceland."

"Now I can forget," Agatha echoed.

"At least for tonight," said Oliveira.

He smiled, but she didn't look at him. Without even looking at him once, she found his flaccid organ in the folds of his

trousers and made it grow, and Oliveira closed his eyes, felt the head moving and the woman's lips confining it. The important thing was Agatha, to keep her company, be with her. This trip south, disguised in the cheap magic of a return to the land of his parents, was not actually anything more than a small private desertion, the act—some would say the cowardice—of a man incapable of living in the place life had assigned him. But now, suddenly, it was taking on a new transcendence. Oliveira had a role in the world and an important position, although momentary, in the life of Agatha, the woman whose tongue he could feel. Here he was safe and the night was safe, too. Here, Oliveira was no longer a threat to himself. He let himself go then and enjoyed doing so, and when he felt himself coming it was as if the night behind him was releasing all its weight, as if the road from Beauvais was repeating over his shoulders in a single instant. Before falling into a deep sleep, he thought of the van and the things inside, and imagined himself emptying his boxes of records on this very bed and organizing them alphabetically in the wardrobe of a long-dead deacon.

He woke up disoriented. He was surrounded by unfamiliar details, and took a while to remember where he was; he was covered by a virgin-wool blanket that made him itch and that he didn't think he'd ever seen before. How long had he been asleep? Long enough, at least, for crusts of sleep to have accumulated in the corners of his eyes, for the weight of his body on top of his arm to have cut off the circulation and a seemingly permanent cramp to appear in his muscles. He held his breath: nothing broke the silence. A warm fresh smell came in from the hallway, a mixture of soap and steam. Only when he stood up did he realize he was barefoot, and in the soles of his feet he felt the creaking of the wooden floors, each uneven board. He found his shoes. His tired feet were swollen, and his shoes were hard to get on. The tape recorder wasn't there.

Oliveira went out into the hall.

"Agatha?"

He got down four steps before noticing that the bathroom door was closed. Then he heard footsteps on the porch, the panel of the mailbox gave a metallic groan, and a plastic envelope slid through the door. On the other side of the frosted glass, Oliveira saw the postman's yellow raincoat turning away. He thought he'd go down and collect her mail and then say good morning to Agatha, and as he bent down to pick up the envelope he felt a pleasant pain in his waist, a tug that was also a call. The transparent envelope contained a magazine about horses, but the subscription label covered the title. Seeing Agatha's name in print for the first time caused a simple and clear emotion. He approached the map on the wall and looked for Iceland. It was a violet-colored country. France, where he still was, was saffron red. Portugal was green, an intense green similar to the color of the van. Abandoning a country was child's play. Swapping colors and not life. Rootlessness had no color, however. It makes no difference to live in one place or another and being born here or there was an accident. One was a chameleon, countries and people mere scenery.

Maybe Agatha would be grateful for an invitation to spend some days with him; maybe she'd even agree to leave with him right now. Oliveira looked for L'Isle-Adam and his index finger traced the route ahead of him, heading for Clermont-Ferrand and arriving in Perpignan and then Barcelona. The skies would be clearer there and it wouldn't be so cold. Next he found the Arctic Circle and followed it around the world through the Bering Strait, as a silent homage to Agatha. She was a brave woman. Over the course of the night she'd faced her phantoms and overcome them. It was almost fascinating: Oliveira now remembered the house where Alma had died, and it was as if a new fear had joined his own. All his life he'd lived with fear, with the sensation of menace. It was absurd. His egotism had protected him; he couldn't feel proud of that. Now he wanted to feel simple emotions. It was a new day and he was hungry.

When he went outside, the dome of clouds had taken on a glassy tone, and the sun was a remote and cold aluminum disk. Perhaps it was the first time that the banal event of a day beginning had given him such satisfaction; it was as if he'd had something to do with it and should be commended. Two doors away from the bakery the air was already smelling of freshly baked bread, a thick and almost visible scent that Oliveira could have cut with his hand. The place was small, but the counter left enough space for a square table and two chairs that looked out from behind the window toward the street. The baker was balder and shorter than he looked before when he was sweeping. His mustache completely hid his lips. The electronic theme music of France 3 came from the back room.

Oliveira pointed to a baguette and asked for two croissants and two *pains au chocolat.*

"And a carton of orange juice," he added.

"No cartons," said the man. "It comes in a bottle, fresh squeezed."

"A bottle, then." Oliveira counted the coins in the palm of his hand. "When would you say dawn has broken? Officially, I mean. When there starts to be light, or only when you can see the sun?"

The man considered the question with a grave expression.

"I would say there are two moments. One is dawn, and one is day. Dawn comes before day."

"So, dawn is before you can see the sun?"

"I'd say so," the man said.

"Dawn comes as soon as the sky is no longer black."

"I think so. Is the lady feeling all right?"

"Do you know her?"

The baker lowered his eyes, feigning prudence.

"From seeing her arrive at this hour," he said. "She never spends the night in her house. But something tells me she's going to be all right from now on. Of course, I'm not minding anybody else's business."

"Of course not," said Oliveira.

He took the package wrapped in thin paper. A croissant flake floated to the floor like a feather.

When he got back to the house, Oliveira went straight into the kitchen. He looked in three cupboards before finding the glasses. They were tall and blue. The window looked out onto a clothesline. A black bra and an apron similar to the one Agatha had used the previous afternoon hung in the breeze. On the paved ground, beside the wall, a box of detergent. A spoonful of white powder had spilled, and seemed to shine on the dirty ground. Oliveira washed down mouthfuls of croissant with big gulps of orange juice. Then, when he decided to take the other croissant up to Agatha, something extraordinary occurred. Maybe it was a quality of the silence, or the image of the lonely, hanging bra and apron. Oliveira began to walk toward the front hallway—without the croissant in his hand—and his footsteps accelerated. He ran up the stairs two at a time. Oliveira tripped on the penultimate step but didn't feel his knee smash into the hard edge. He opened the bathroom door without knocking, maybe because he already knew. Naked, Agatha was sleeping in the bathtub; Oliveira found the waterline, level with her shoulders and just covering her breast, and saw her relaxed nipples almost at the same time as he saw the first cloud of blood, supple and round like a balloon coming away from the bottom of a swimming pool.

Oliveira called her and heard the echo of his voice. He sprang to her side and his first instinct was to take her by the wrists, pull her hands out of the water to prevent the gentle and efficient and dreadful emptying of her open veins. The tip of his index finger slipped momentarily into her viscous flesh: Agatha had made too deep a cut. He felt a weak pulse, reluctant but existent, a slight palpitation in her thumb. She was alive, it was still possible to save her. The air floating above the mixture of water and blood had a rusty taste. Oliveira knelt down to get his arms under her body. His shirt-sleeves absorbed a pastel red. The cuffs were as heavy as sponges. He found that her body was lighter than he'd imagined and the water, instead of making her slippery, increased the friction between Agatha's skin and his own. His heart was shuddering at the base of his throat. His own blood pounded in his temples. Oliveira felt a second of intense panic and knew he had never known such a sensation and also knew that nightmares are made of the same stuff as this moment. He wanted to stand up and carry Agatha out of the house and take her to a hospital. He wanted to make a phone call and, while waiting for the men who would arrive among strident sirens, apply a tourniquet over those little-girl bones, though he didn't know how. He wanted to move, do something for the woman who was dying, anything. But his body would not obey.

He closed his eyes as if praying. A single image illuminated his mind: the tiny shadow of the lizard he'd seen before Agatha started telling him about Grímsey Island, where it was always sunny and people had no pasts or guilt, where life was not a burden. Now he knew that the most diligent team of doctors, the most urgent attention could not save this woman, because her pain was not in the yellow skin of her wrists or the scalpel cuts, and she would still be tormented every night even if they replaced all the blood she had lost today. Oliveira looked at her pale face, mouth half open, her soaked forehead as if in the grip of a violent fever. He didn't feel resentment, although it now seemed like Agatha was abandoning him; he didn't see a woman who perhaps, with more time, he could have loved, but a body at rest, redeemed and free, so ostentatious in her liberty that only nudity seemed to suit her. At last she sleeps, thought Oliveira. Love, which he'd so often heard about in abstract terms or tacky images, could be this simple: Agatha fleeing and the will to not prevent her flight.

Oliveira took his arms out of the tainted water. The body sank a little, making small waves on the surface, and ended up settling like a bottle. The stream of blood was saffron dust on the bottom of the bathtub, the ink of an escaping octopus. Clumsily Oliveira turned around, leaned his back against the edge of the tub, and stayed there, sitting on the carpet that gave the bathroom a tasteless or outmoded look. His eyes registered the pattern in the wallpaper, the back of the toilet like a beer stein, and the fiberglass counter, where the tape recorder rested beside the bottle of Xylocaine, and then he felt an emptiness in his stomach, something like the inability to catch your breath after a blow, as he understood that this woman had even wanted to avoid the pain of the blade slicing her skin: Agatha had been afraid, afraid of the pain, perhaps afraid of what she would feel when she started to die. Beneath the blade of the scalpel, the same one she'd used to emasculate a purebred stallion, the black drop, dense and solitary, reminded Oliveira of the English wax his father had used to seal his love letters, whether or not they were addressed to his mother.

FROM THE SECOND FLOOR Oliveira could see the street was beginning to show signs of life. A green and blue bus went past, the white interior lights still on, and stopped to drop off a passenger. The door opened and a woman of about fifty stepped down, her hair freshly washed, straightening her dress with her hands. Her day was just starting. Oliveira's eyes followed her until she turned the corner, thirty meters beyond the door to the bakery.

He didn't want to think he'd failed her. He wondered if Agatha had thought of him before or after opening her veins, or if she hadn't considered his presence at all, if after all he'd been nothing more than that evening's one-night stand. Maybe he had failed her. Maybe he'd had in his hands and in his voice the way to prevent Agatha's death. But how could he have imagined the effects a word, a subtle lie, might have had on her? Maybe Agatha had made the decision long before that night, and nothing Oliveira might have said would have changed it. Maybe his presence was only required as a witness. He wondered if that was true: if everything had a human cause and another random one, if destiny existed. He also wondered if Agatha had crossed herself, if she'd listened for one last time to her daughter's voice, if a woman who has decided to die allows herself the luxury of sentimentalism or the nostalgia of faith. A man holding a little boy's hand walks past on the other side of the street. The boy carries a knapsack wider than his own back. They do not know that here, in this house, so close to them, a woman has suffered. It's good that they don't know, especially the boy. "From seeing her arrive at this hour," the baker had said. Agatha formed part of a street's waking routine. The baker, the boy, Agatha. Three islands, and Oliveira just another island. Maybe communication between two people was never possible, or it was possible but imperfect, and its imperfections were capable of ending a life. There was no way of knowing. Two big drops burst against the windowpane, almost at once. Then it began to rain. Oliveira felt cold in his eyes and a sort of uncomfortable sting. It was lucky it was raining because people who looked at his eyes would think of raindrops before anything else.

His knee hurt. But, no matter how hard he tried, he could not remember when he'd banged it. He turned around, looked at the bathroom door, and didn't remember having chosen to close it, either.

V

"Coffee," said Oliveira. "A strong one."

He was sitting beside the window. On the table was Agatha's magazine, open in the middle. Beside the magazine, folded neatly, was the map of the world. Oliveira had taken it down off the wall and as he pulled out one of the thumbtacks he'd torn the flesh under his fingernail. The baker spoke to him from behind the counter.

"Have you made up your mind yet, monsieur?"

"Pardon?"

"Whether dawn breaks before or after. Look, *chérie*, it's him. Monsieur wanted to know about the sun, what I told you about."

"*Ah oui,*" said the woman. She had freckles on her rosy cheeks and her hair up in an impeccable bun. "My husband told me about that, it's very interesting. So many things out there and one never stops to think about them. It's . . . it's unfair."

"Monsieur arrived with madame," said the baker.

His wife knew immediately who he meant.

"That's very good." She smiled. "Yes, definitely. This is good news."

Then the woman went into a room where two columns of baking sheets guarded the door frame like shelves. She took a tray from one and put it on the other. "*C'est une bonne nouvelle,*" she said. "I knew it. One day someone just had to come."

The baker placed a cup of coffee on top of the folded map. He lowered his voice and leaned forward, a man peering over a precipice. His tone was more than cordial: it was warm, almost affectionate.

"Monsieur is well? Do you feel ill? My wife can bring you something if your eyes are stinging, monsieur."

"I'm fine. Thank you."

"It's probably the pollution. The clouds bring us all the pollution from Paris. It's very hard on the eyes."

"Of course."

"Drops, monsieur. In any pharmacy. You shouldn't drive with your eyes so irritated."

"You're right. Excuse me. I have to get going."

"Monsieur is traveling? Will you be away long?"

"Not that it's any of your business, but yes, I do have to make a trip."

The baker did not insist. Oliveira had been rude to him and on his face appeared a glimmer of disenchantment. Maybe he'd been too abrupt, thought Oliveira, and regretted it, but it was too late now. He was grateful for the coffee, the bitter taste on his tongue. It was still raining. Oliveira couldn't wait any longer. He put a five-franc coin in the ashtray and collected up his papers in one hand.

"Monsieur doesn't have to leave," said the baker. "You can stay without ordering anything."

"Say good-bye to your wife for me," said Oliveira.

"Good luck, monsieur."

"Thank you. Could you do me a favor?"

"Yes, monsieur."

"Take Agatha . . . take the lady a bag of coffee. A gift from me. She's sleeping right now, but take it to her later."

The baker smiled. He looked at Agatha's house and then looked back at Oliveira.

"Yes, monsieur. With pleasure, monsieur."

THE VAN WAS RESTING beside the curb like an anesthetized horse. To Oliveira it seemed like a useless, obsolete, almost despicable machine. I've waited with you, Agatha, I've accompanied you to the end of the night. He started the engine and waited for the thin layer of ice on the windshield to melt. His eyes began to water and the interior of the vehicle was a hazy vision. Oliveira squeezed his eyelids and one fat tear fell onto the steering wheel. Then others formed in his eyes, as if they were trying to dissolve his perception of things or at least delay his departure. He was surprised by an idea: if his life ended now—if a drunk driver plowed into him from behind and broke his neck, if a man driven crazy by grief came out shooting randomly—his years of living would have served for nothing. Who would he be, who might he have been? He would be the man who abandoned the only land he could call his own; he would be the man who allowed a woman to die.

He didn't do any calculations but knew he was running late. He had to get going, continue to make his way south, past the Pyrenees and drive several more hours after that. He had two days ahead of him. After that, his parents' city, whose name had no meaning whatsoever and in which Oliveira had never lived, would welcome him. He couldn't imagine his future life, or what his friends would be like or what they'd look like. But he would begin to live a different life and was somehow liberated and ready to respond to the change. There would be a woman. Oliveira would look at her every once in a while and think: You are her. I've chosen you. You've chosen me. But that woman didn't have a face, and wasn't expecting him, and could not know that her life, in that instant, was beginning to be different because Oliveira was traveling toward her. He himself would be until the moment of arrival somewhat uncertain, a malleable substance, vulnerable to words and weather and the portent of love, a body in movement across a map, less alone than before, crossing meridians.